THE HARDY BOYS

UNDERCOVER BROTHERS™

PAPERCUTZ™

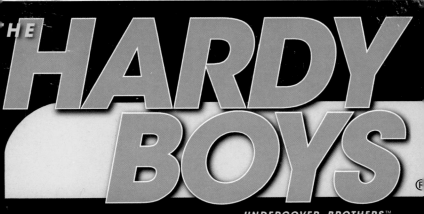

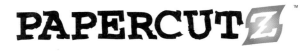

THE HARDY BOYS®

UNDERCOVER BROTHERS™

Graphic Novels
Available from Papercutz

#1 The Ocean of Osyria
#2 Identity Theft
(coming July 2005)
#3 Mad House
(coming November 2005)

$7.95 each in paperback
$12.95 each in hardcover

ALL NEW STORY ALL NEW GRAPHIC NOVEL
THE HARDY BOYS®
#2 IDENTITY THEFT
UNDERCOVER BROTHERS
Scott LOBDELL
Daniel RENDON
based on the novels of Franklin W. Dixon
PAPERCUTZ

ALL NEW STORY ALL NEW GRAPHIC NOVEL
THE HARDY BOYS®
#3 MAD HOUSE
UNDERCOVER BROTHERS
Scott LOBDELL
Daniel RENDON
based on the novels of Franklin W. Dixon
MaD HOuSE
PAPERCUTZ

Add $3 P&H for 1st item, $1 each addt'l.
Send for our catalog:
Papercutz
555 Eighth Avenue, Suite 1202
New York, NY 10018
www.papercutz.com

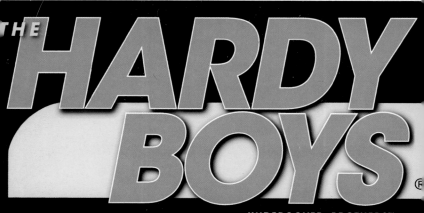

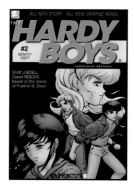

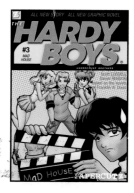

THE HARDY BOYS

BOYS

#1

UNDERCOVER BROTHERS™

The Ocean of Osyria

SCOTT LOBDELL • Writer
LEA HERNANDEZ • Artist
preview art by DANIEL RENDON
Based on the series by
FRANKLIN W. DIXON

PAPERCUTZ™

New York

The Ocean of Oysyria
SCOTT LOBDELL – Writer
LEA HERNANDEZ – Artist
BRYAN SENKA – Letterer
LOVERN KINDZIERSKI – Colorist
JIM SALICRUP
Editor-in-Chief

ISBN 1-59707-001-7 paperback edition
ISBN 1-59707-005-X hardcover edition

10   9   8   7   6   5   4   3   2   1

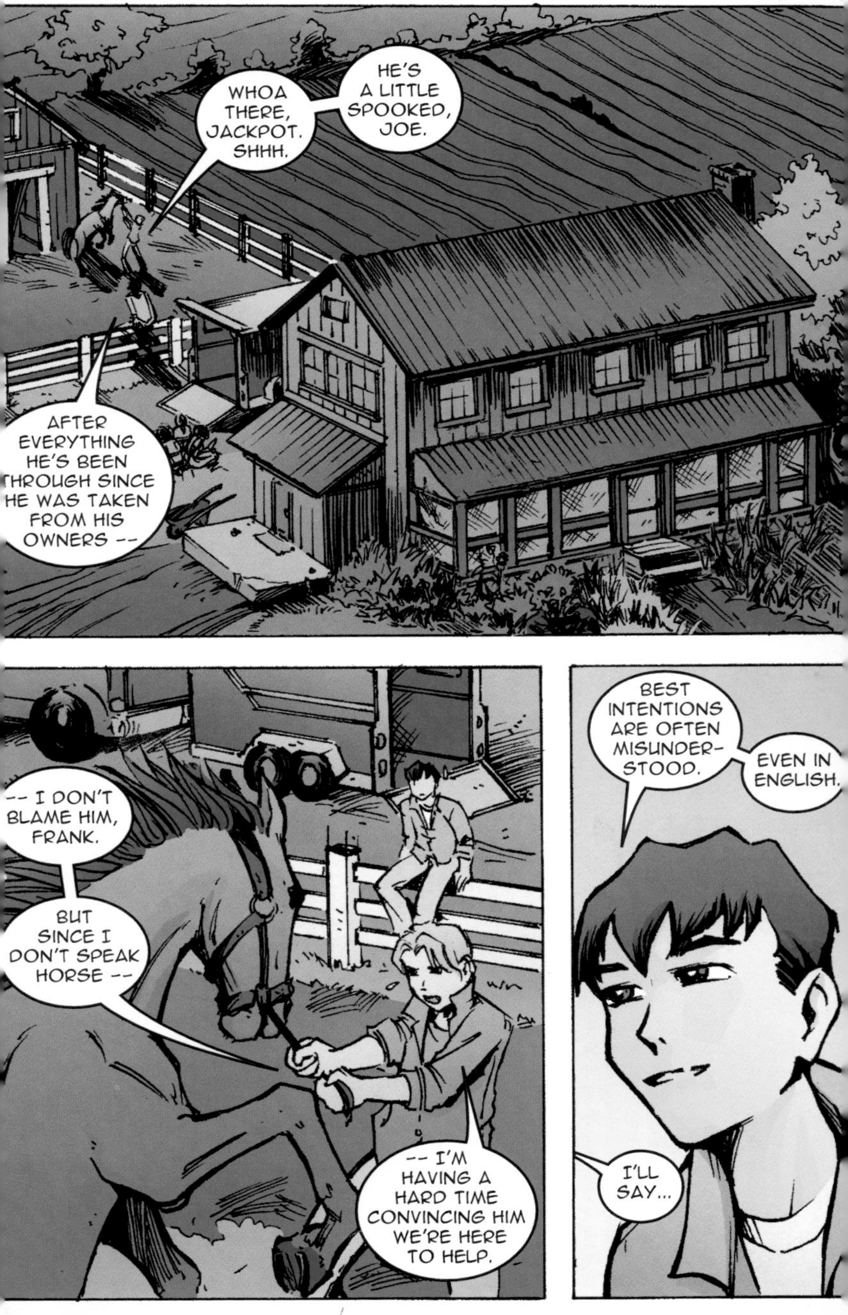
WHOA THERE, JACKPOT. SHHH.
HE'S A LITTLE SPOOKED, JOE.
AFTER EVERYTHING HE'S BEEN THROUGH SINCE HE WAS TAKEN FROM HIS OWNERS --
-- I DON'T BLAME HIM, FRANK.
BUT SINCE I DON'T SPEAK HORSE --
-- I'M HAVING A HARD TIME CONVINCING HIM WE'RE HERE TO HELP.
BEST INTENTIONS ARE OFTEN MISUNDER-STOOD.
EVEN IN ENGLISH.
I'LL SAY...

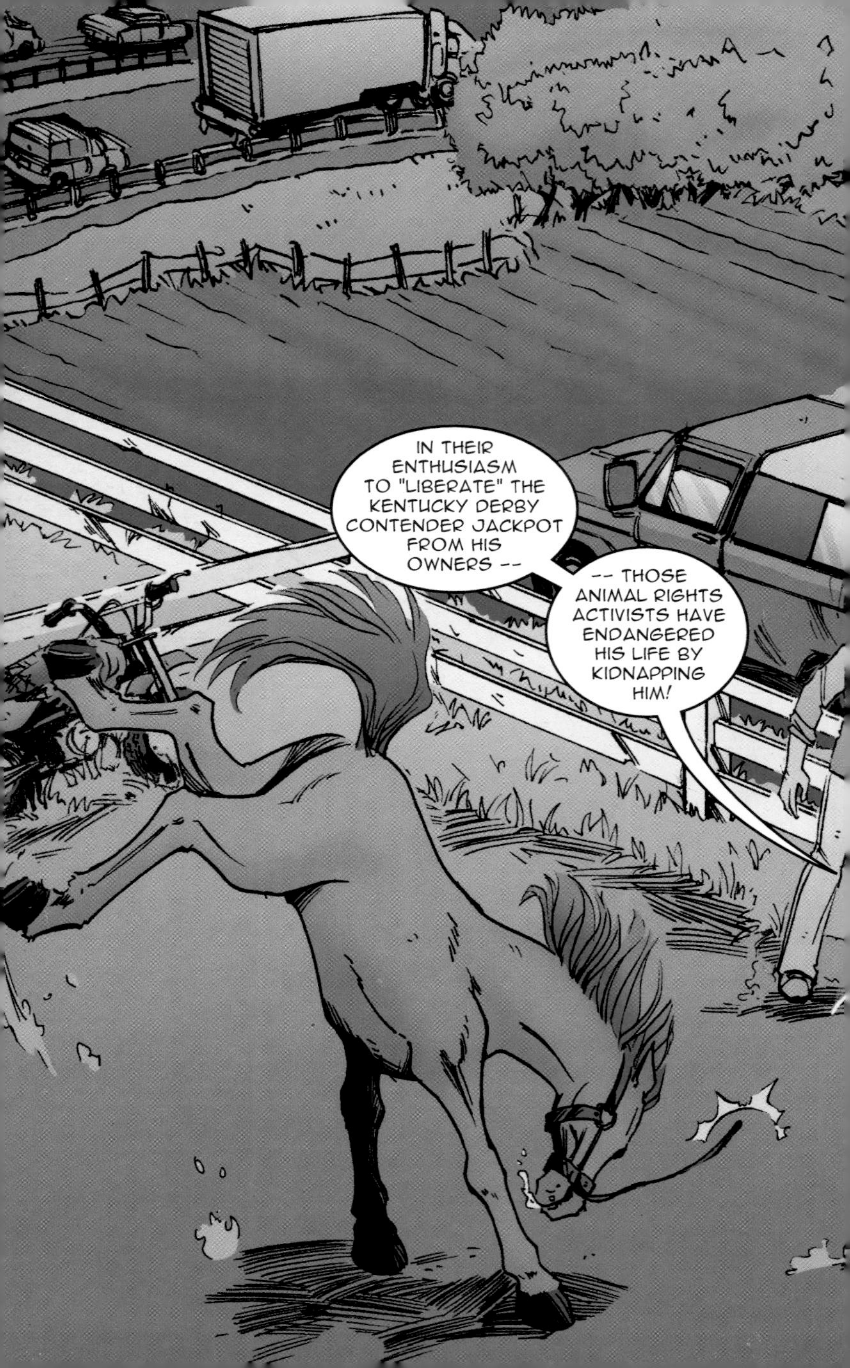
IN THEIR ENTHUSIASM TO "LIBERATE" THE KENTUCKY DERBY CONTENDER JACKPOT FROM HIS OWNERS --
-- THOSE ANIMAL RIGHTS ACTIVISTS HAVE ENDANGERED HIS LIFE BY KIDNAPPING HIM!

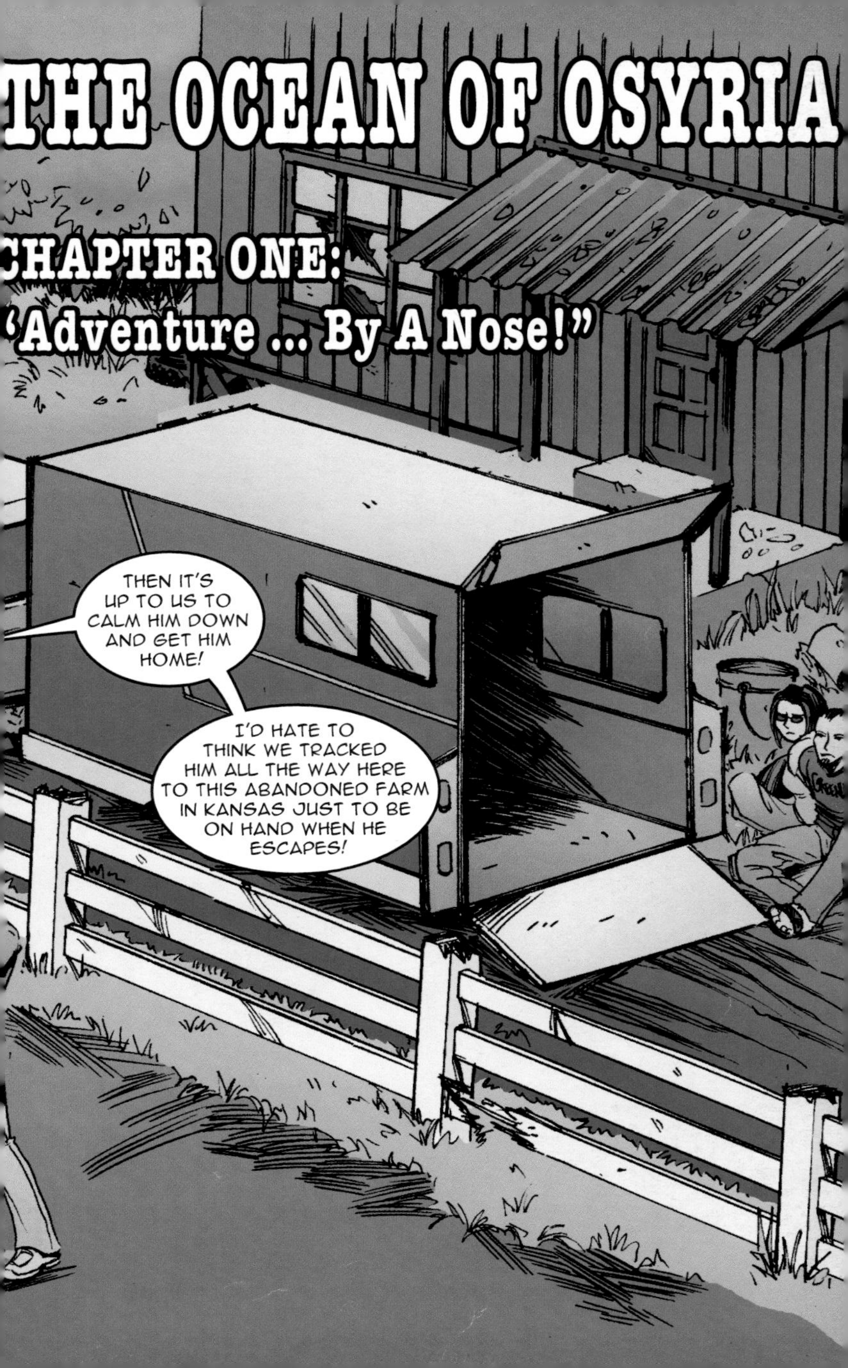
THE OCEAN OF OSYRIA
CHAPTER ONE:
"Adventure ... By A Nose!"
THEN IT'S UP TO US TO CALM HIM DOWN AND GET HIM HOME!
I'D HATE TO THINK WE TRACKED HIM ALL THE WAY HERE TO THIS ABANDONED FARM IN KANSAS JUST TO BE ON HAND WHEN HE ESCAPES!

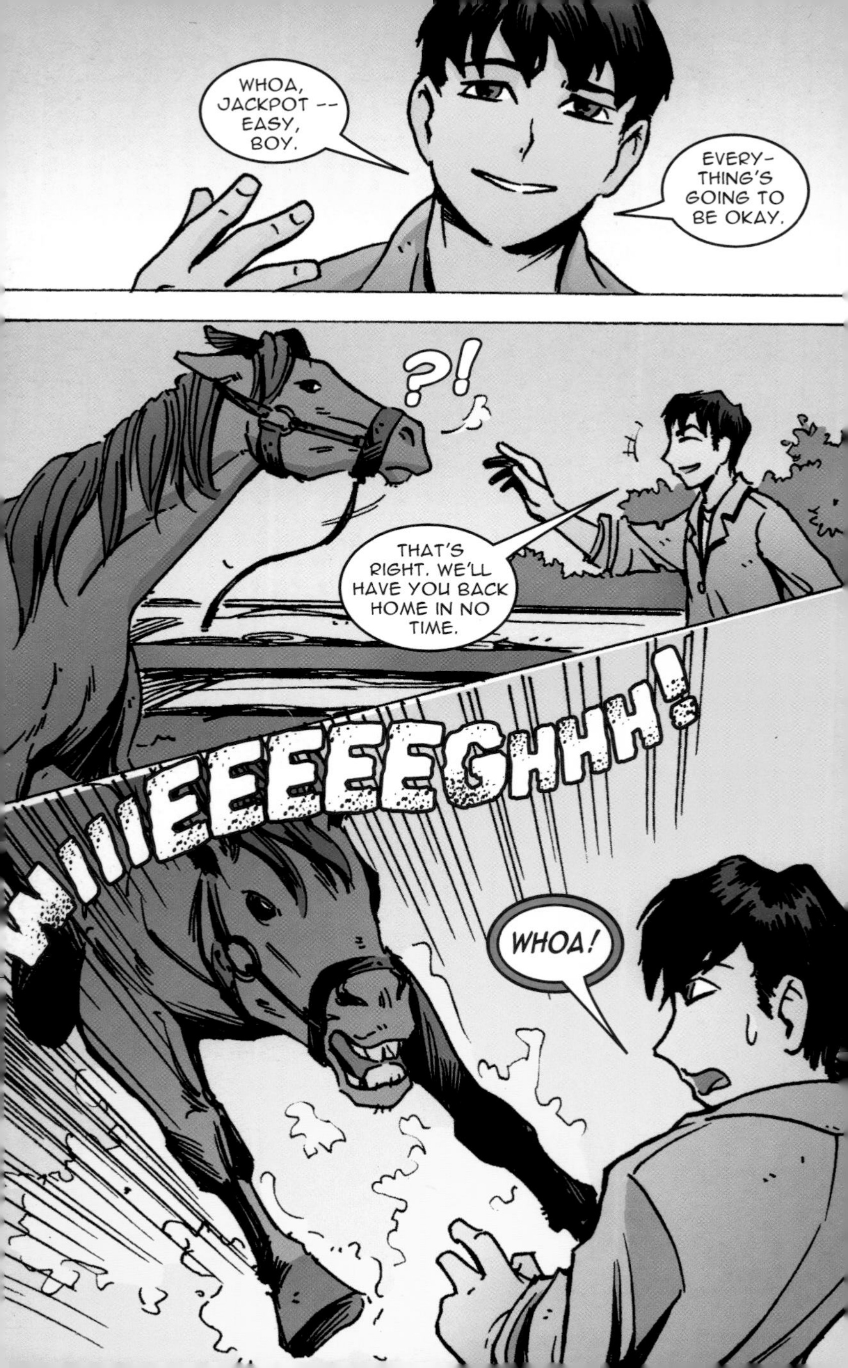
WHOA, JACKPOT -- EASY, BOY.
EVERY-THING'S GOING TO BE OKAY.
?!
THAT'S RIGHT. WE'LL HAVE YOU BACK HOME IN NO TIME.
WHIIEEEEEGHHH!
WHOA!

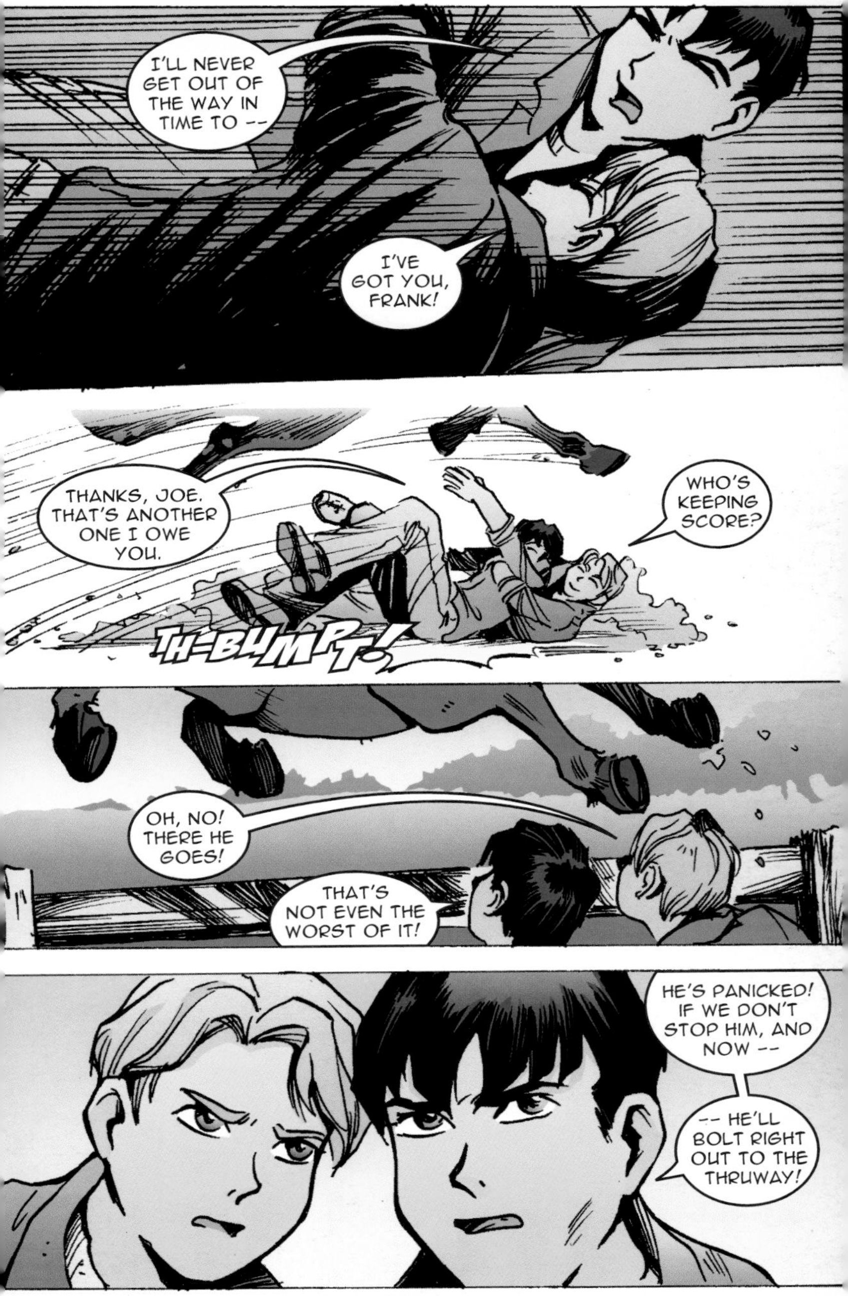
I'LL NEVER GET OUT OF THE WAY IN TIME TO --
I'VE GOT YOU, FRANK!
THANKS, JOE. THAT'S ANOTHER ONE I OWE YOU.
WHO'S KEEPING SCORE?
TH-BUMPT!
OH, NO! THERE HE GOES!
THAT'S NOT EVEN THE WORST OF IT!
HE'S PANICKED! IF WE DON'T STOP HIM, AND NOW --
-- HE'LL BOLT RIGHT OUT TO THE THRUWAY!

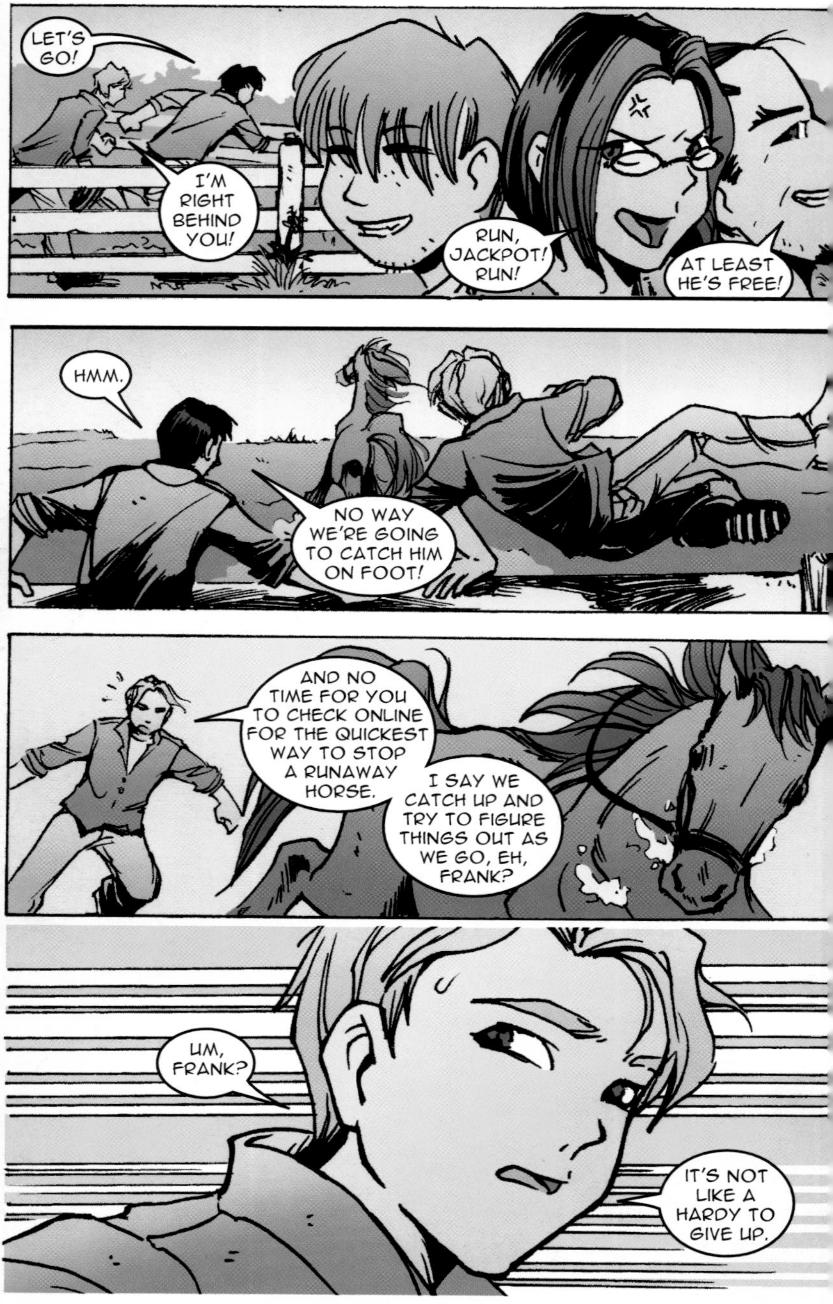
LET'S GO!
I'M RIGHT BEHIND YOU!
RUN, JACKPOT! RUN!
AT LEAST HE'S FREE!
HMM.
NO WAY WE'RE GOING TO CATCH HIM ON FOOT!
AND NO TIME FOR YOU TO CHECK ONLINE FOR THE QUICKEST WAY TO STOP A RUNAWAY HORSE.
I SAY WE CATCH UP AND TRY TO FIGURE THINGS OUT AS WE GO, EH, FRANK?
UM, FRANK?
IT'S NOT LIKE A HARDY TO GIVE UP.

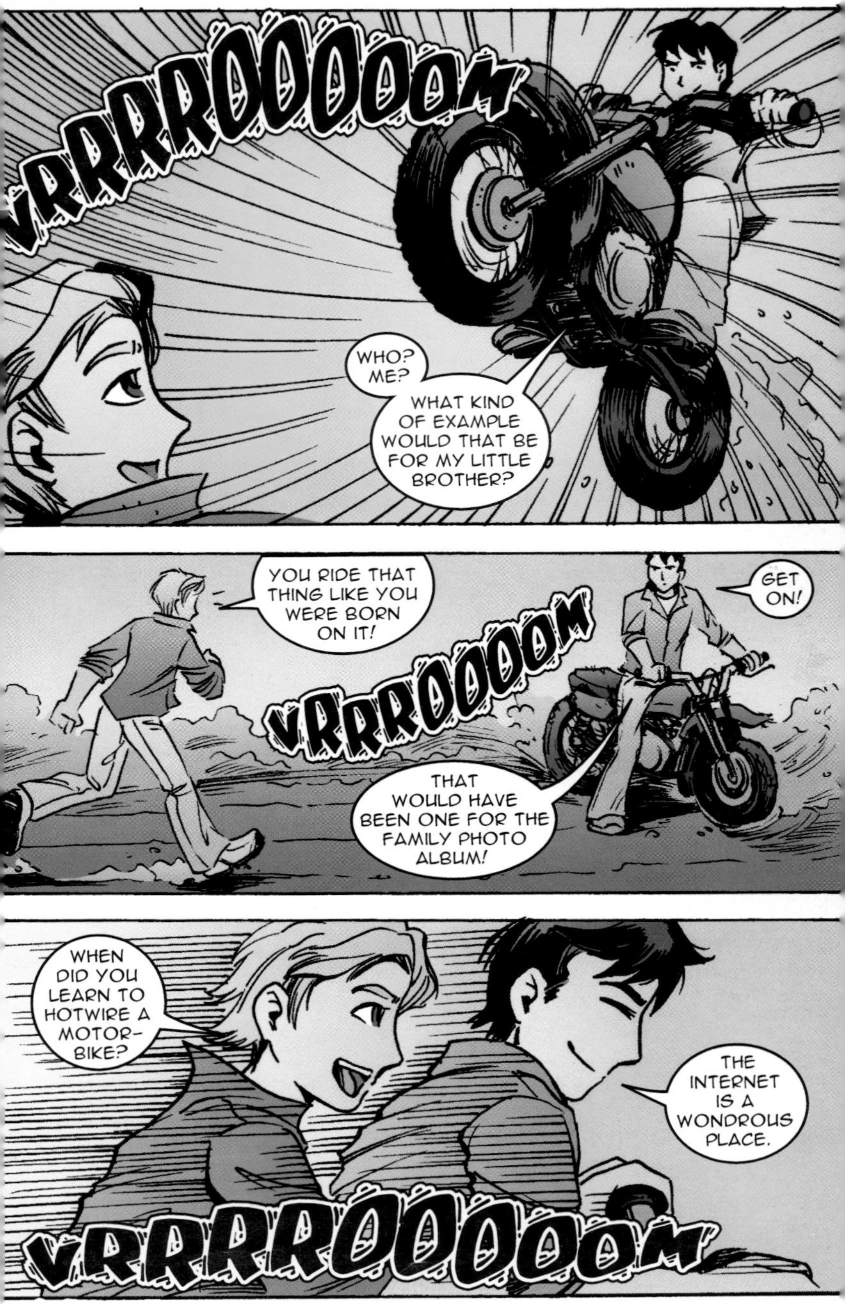
VRRRROOOOOOM
WHO? ME?
WHAT KIND OF EXAMPLE WOULD THAT BE FOR MY LITTLE BROTHER?
YOU RIDE THAT THING LIKE YOU WERE BORN ON IT!
GET ON!
VRRROOOOOM
THAT WOULD HAVE BEEN ONE FOR THE FAMILY PHOTO ALBUM!
WHEN DID YOU LEARN TO HOTWIRE A MOTOR-BIKE?
THE INTERNET IS A WONDROUS PLACE.
VRRRROOOOOOM

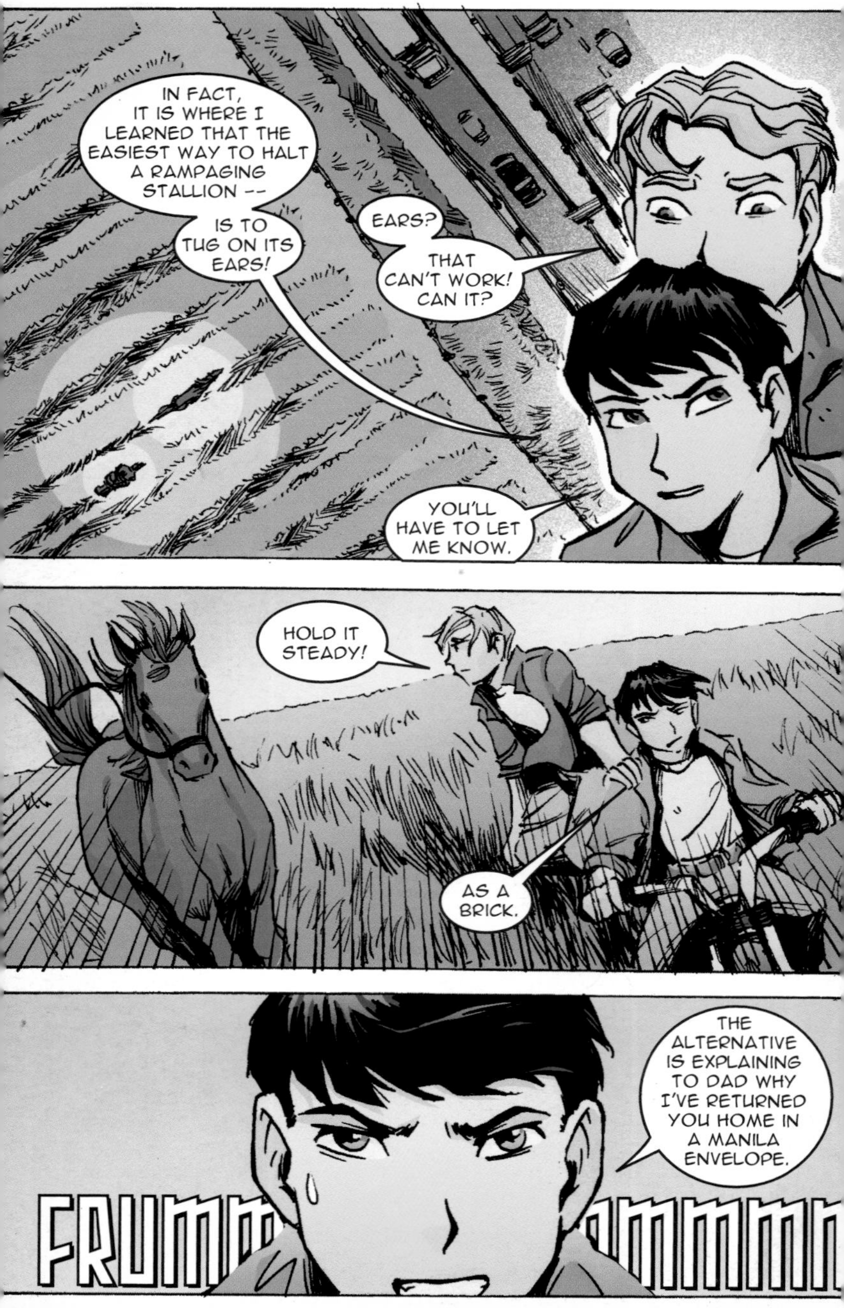
IN FACT, IT IS WHERE I LEARNED THAT THE EASIEST WAY TO HALT A RAMPAGING STALLION --
IS TO TUG ON ITS EARS!
EARS?
THAT CAN'T WORK! CAN IT?
YOU'LL HAVE TO LET ME KNOW.
HOLD IT STEADY!
AS A BRICK.
THE ALTERNATIVE IS EXPLAINING TO DAD WHY I'VE RETURNED YOU HOME IN A MANILA ENVELOPE.
FRUMMMMMMMMMM

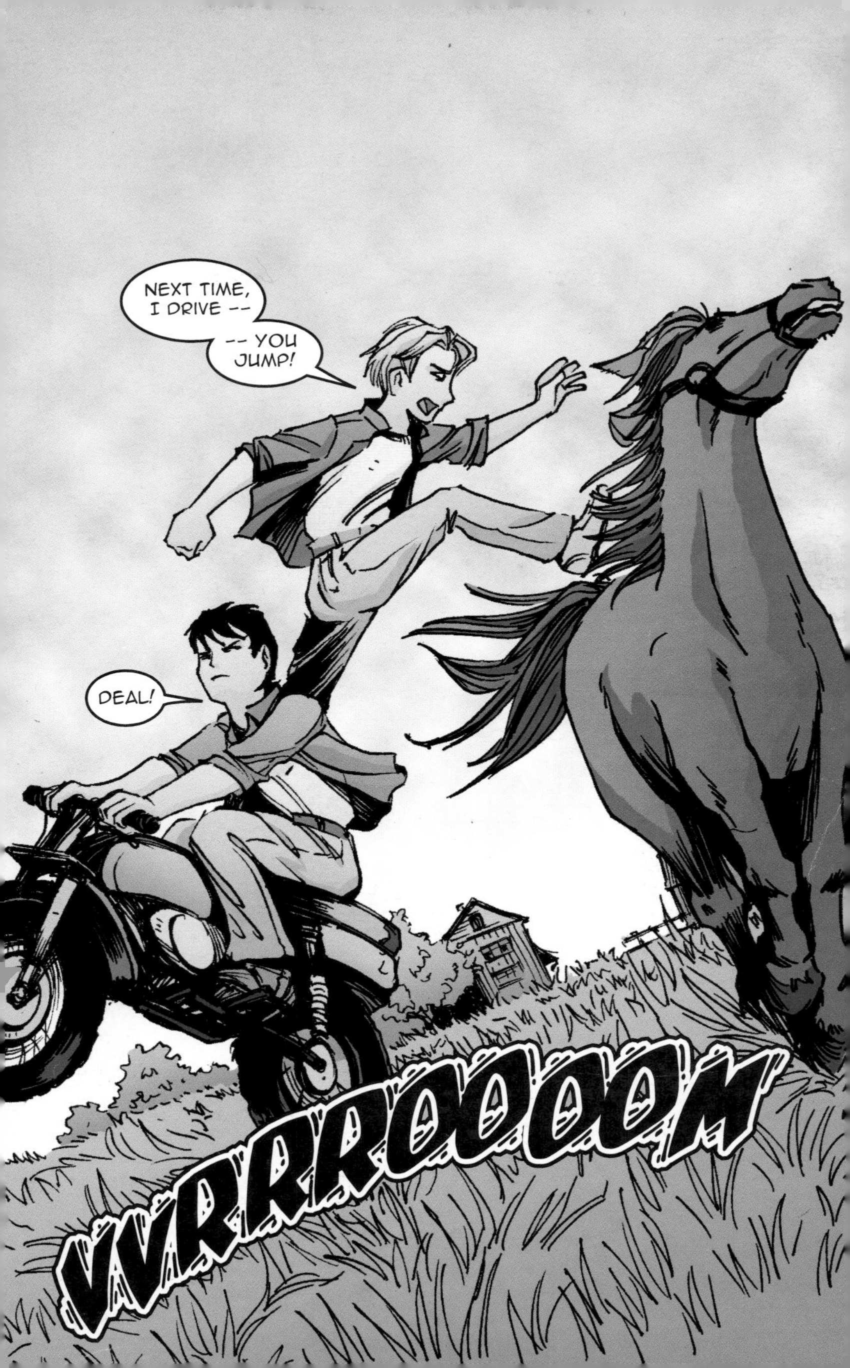
NEXT TIME, I DRIVE --
-- YOU JUMP!
DEAL!
VVRRROOOOM

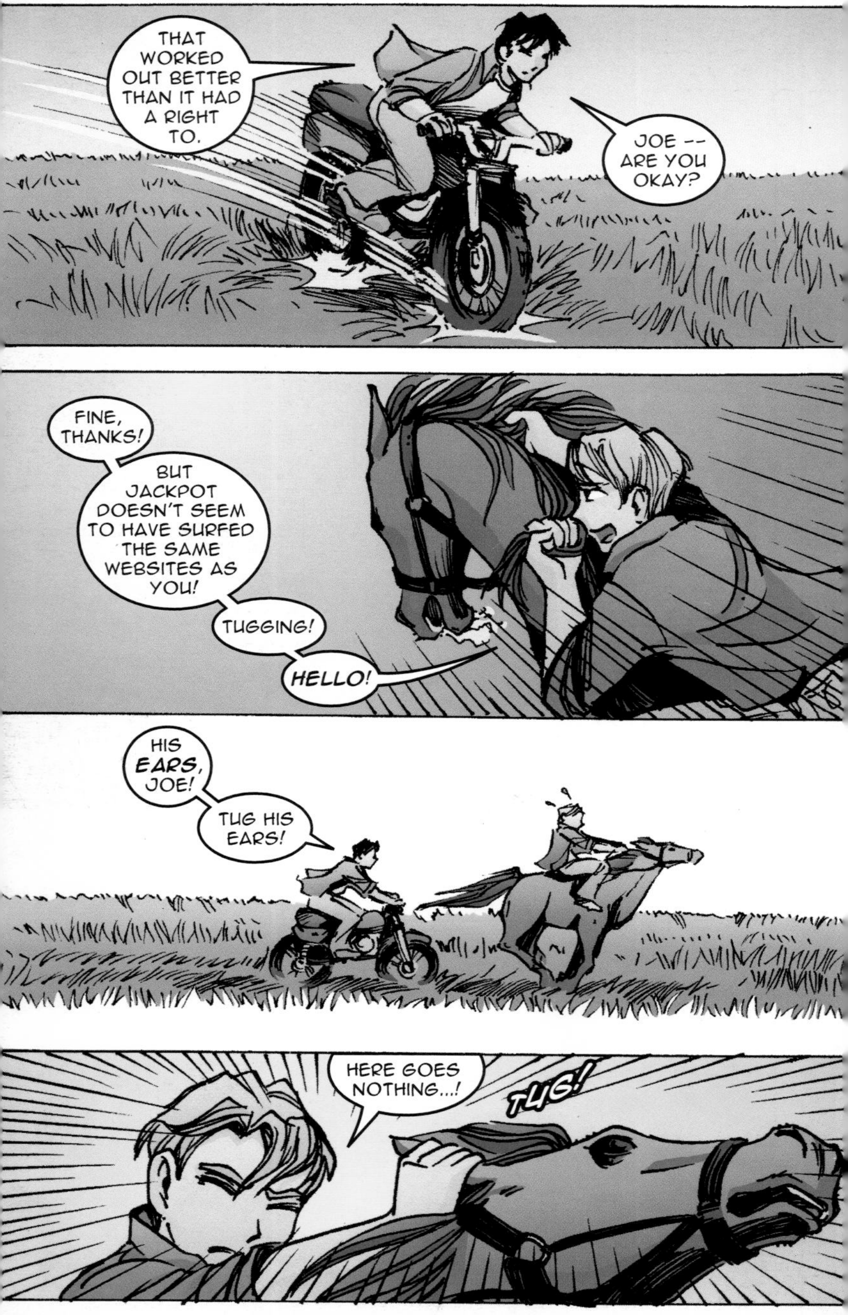
THAT WORKED OUT BETTER THAN IT HAD A RIGHT TO.
JOE -- ARE YOU OKAY?
FINE, THANKS!
BUT JACKPOT DOESN'T SEEM TO HAVE SURFED THE SAME WEBSITES AS YOU!
TUGGING!
HELLO!
HIS EARS, JOE!
TUG HIS EARS!
HERE GOES NOTHING...!
TUG!

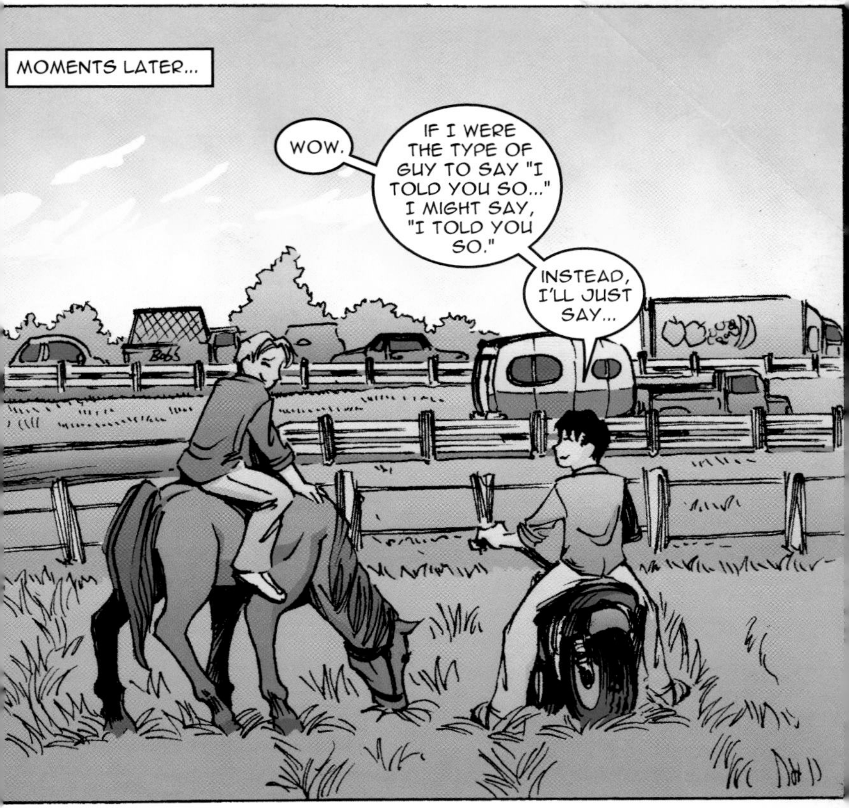
MOMENTS LATER...
WOW.
IF I WERE THE TYPE OF GUY TO SAY "I TOLD YOU SO..." I MIGHT SAY, "I TOLD YOU SO."
INSTEAD, I'LL JUST SAY...

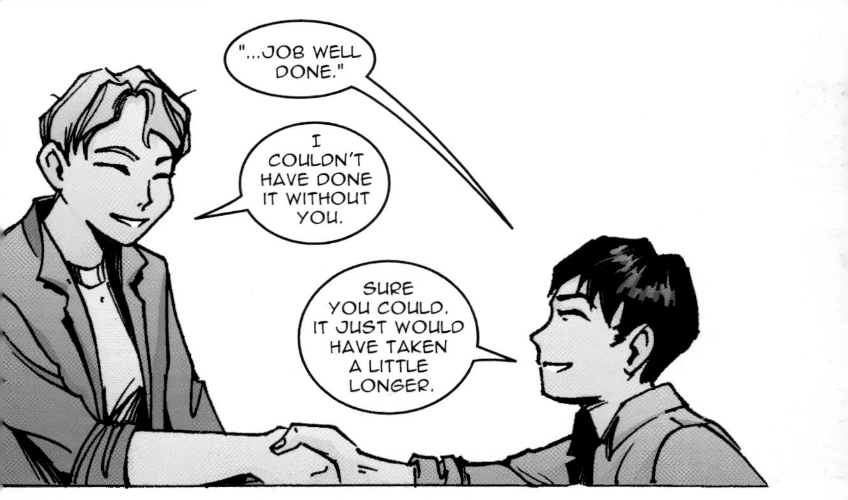
"...JOB WELL DONE."
I COULDN'T HAVE DONE IT WITHOUT YOU.
SURE YOU COULD. IT JUST WOULD HAVE TAKEN A LITTLE LONGER.

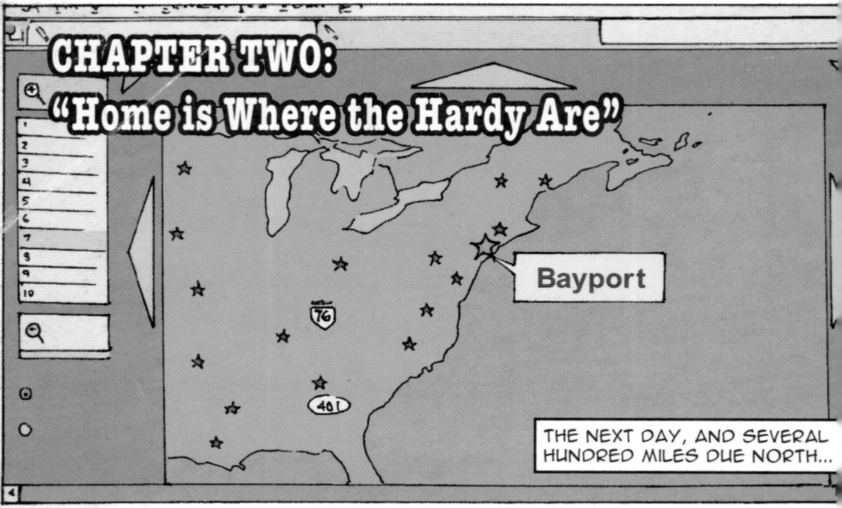
CHAPTER TWO:
"Home is Where the Hardy Are"
Bayport
76
401
THE NEXT DAY, AND SEVERAL HUNDRED MILES DUE NORTH...

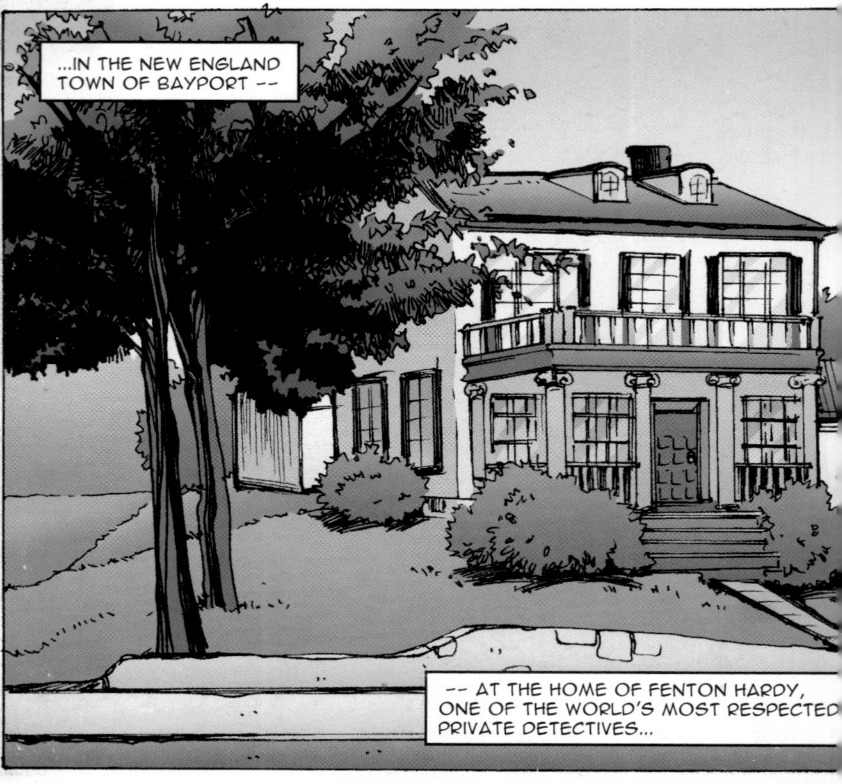
...IN THE NEW ENGLAND TOWN OF BAYPORT --
-- AT THE HOME OF FENTON HARDY, ONE OF THE WORLD'S MOST RESPECTED PRIVATE DETECTIVES...

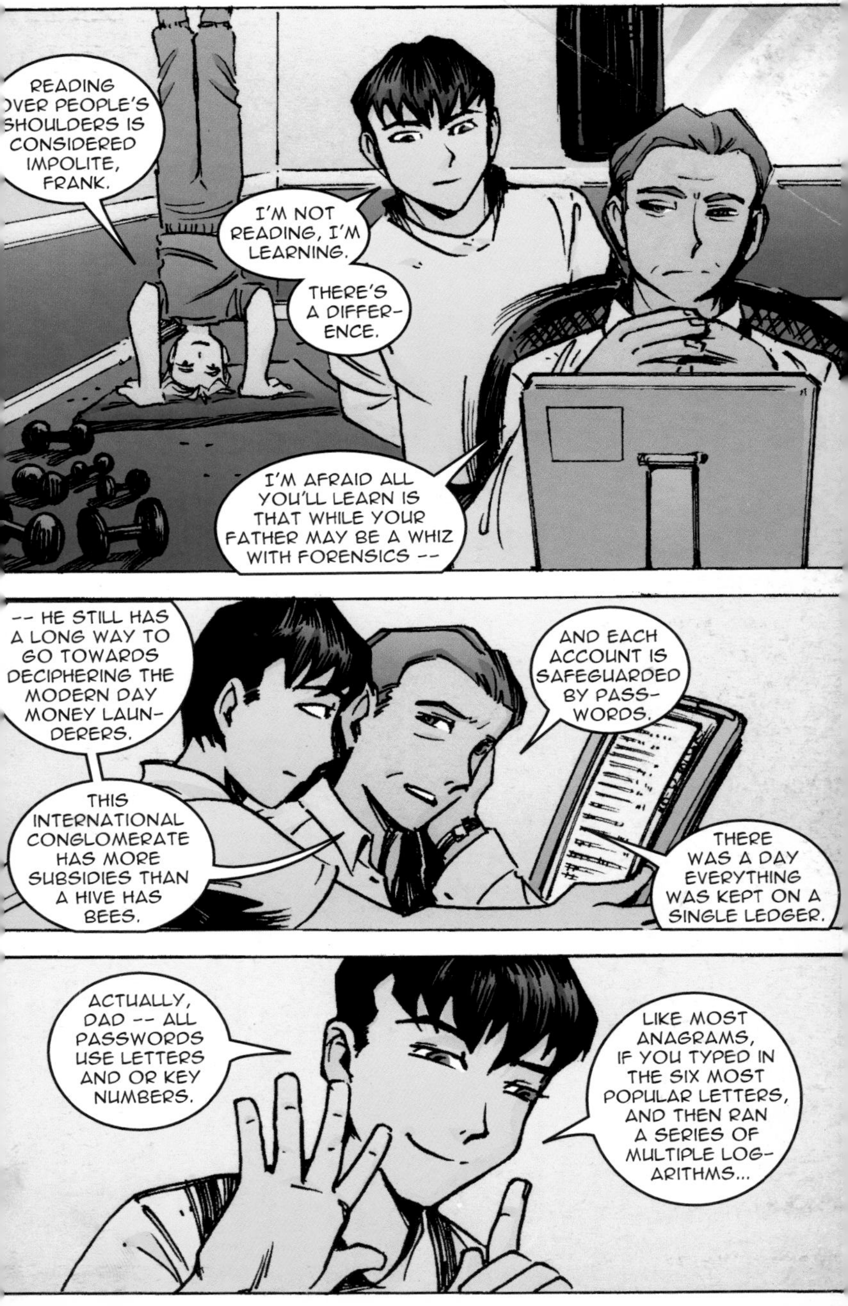
READING OVER PEOPLE'S SHOULDERS IS CONSIDERED IMPOLITE, FRANK.
I'M NOT READING, I'M LEARNING.
THERE'S A DIFFER-ENCE.
I'M AFRAID ALL YOU'LL LEARN IS THAT WHILE YOUR FATHER MAY BE A WHIZ WITH FORENSICS --
-- HE STILL HAS A LONG WAY TO GO TOWARDS DECIPHERING THE MODERN DAY MONEY LAUN-DERERS.
THIS INTERNATIONAL CONGLOMERATE HAS MORE SUBSIDIES THAN A HIVE HAS BEES.
AND EACH ACCOUNT IS SAFEGUARDED BY PASS-WORDS.
THERE WAS A DAY EVERYTHING WAS KEPT ON A SINGLE LEDGER.
ACTUALLY, DAD -- ALL PASSWORDS USE LETTERS AND OR KEY NUMBERS.
LIKE MOST ANAGRAMS, IF YOU TYPED IN THE SIX MOST POPULAR LETTERS, AND THEN RAN A SERIES OF MULTIPLE LOG-ARITHMS...

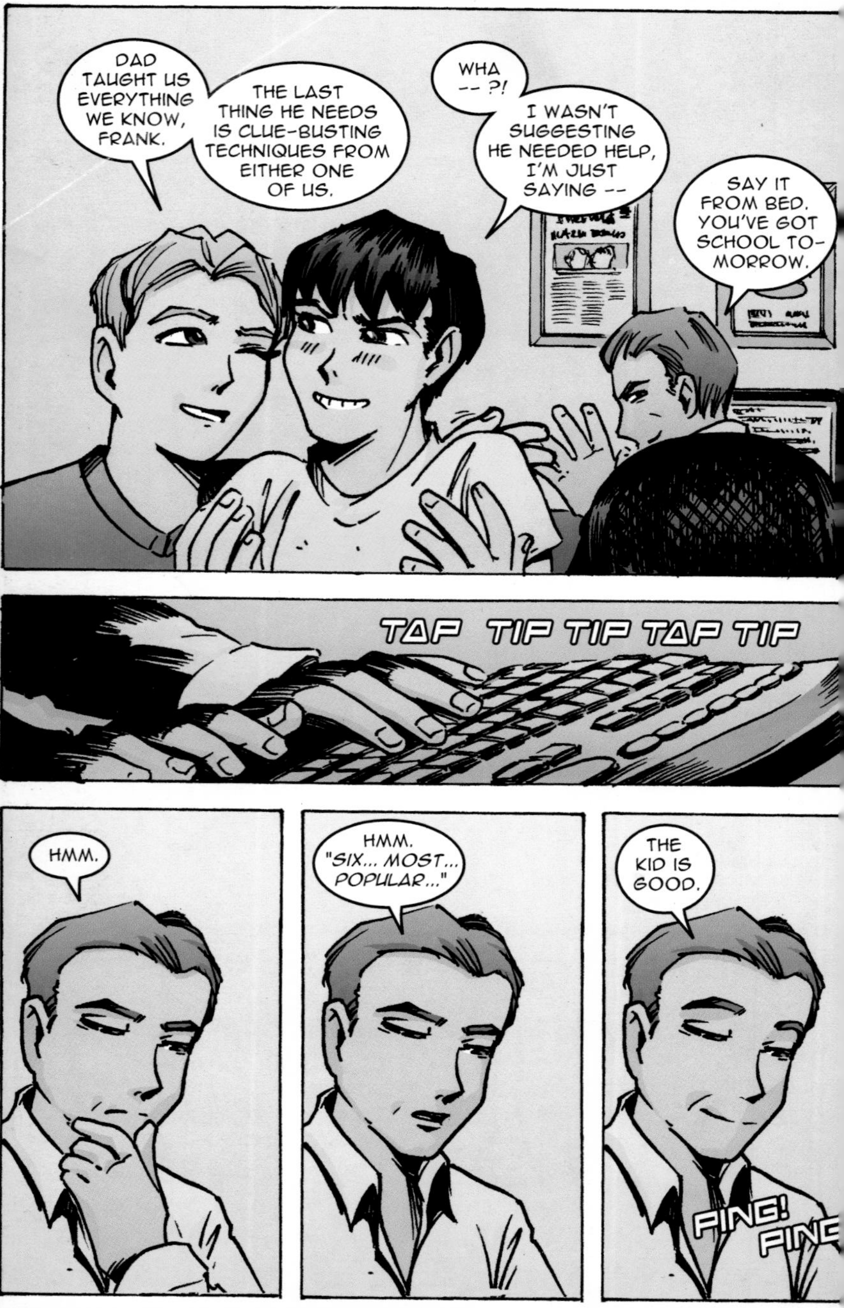
DAD TAUGHT US EVERYTHING WE KNOW, FRANK.
THE LAST THING HE NEEDS IS CLUE-BUSTING TECHNIQUES FROM EITHER ONE OF US.
WHA -- ?!
I WASN'T SUGGESTING HE NEEDED HELP, I'M JUST SAYING --
SAY IT FROM BED. YOU'VE GOT SCHOOL TO-MORROW.
TAP TIP TIP TAP TIP
HMM.
HMM. "SIX... MOST... POPULAR..."
THE KID IS GOOD.
FING! FING

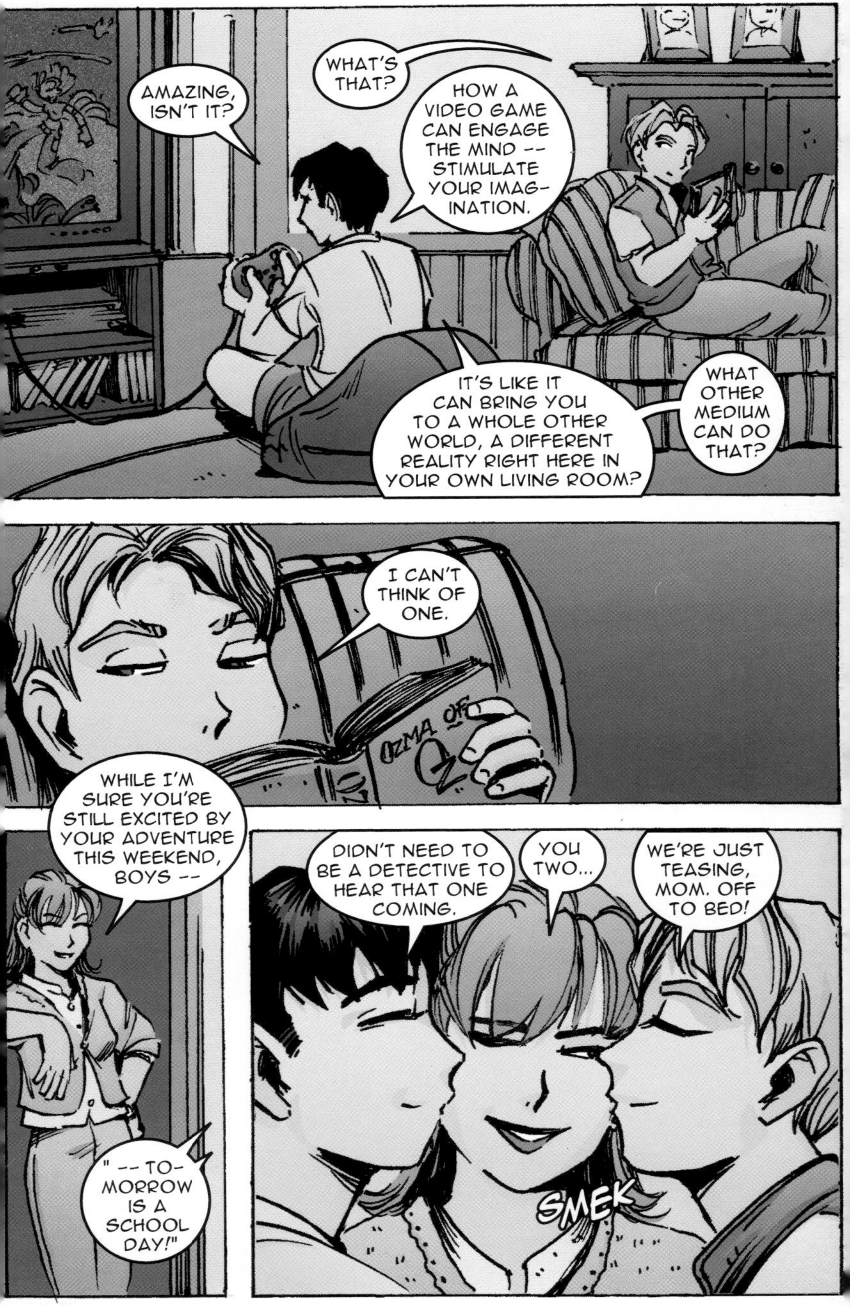
AMAZING, ISN'T IT?
WHAT'S THAT?
HOW A VIDEO GAME CAN ENGAGE THE MIND -- STIMULATE YOUR IMAG- INATION.
IT'S LIKE IT CAN BRING YOU TO A WHOLE OTHER WORLD, A DIFFERENT REALITY RIGHT HERE IN YOUR OWN LIVING ROOM?
WHAT OTHER MEDIUM CAN DO THAT?
I CAN'T THINK OF ONE.
OZMA OF OZ
WHILE I'M SURE YOU'RE STILL EXCITED BY YOUR ADVENTURE THIS WEEKEND, BOYS --
" -- TO- MORROW IS A SCHOOL DAY!"
DIDN'T NEED TO BE A DETECTIVE TO HEAR THAT ONE COMING.
YOU TWO...
WE'RE JUST TEASING, MOM. OFF TO BED!
SMEK

CHAPTER THREE:
"First Class ... Danger!"

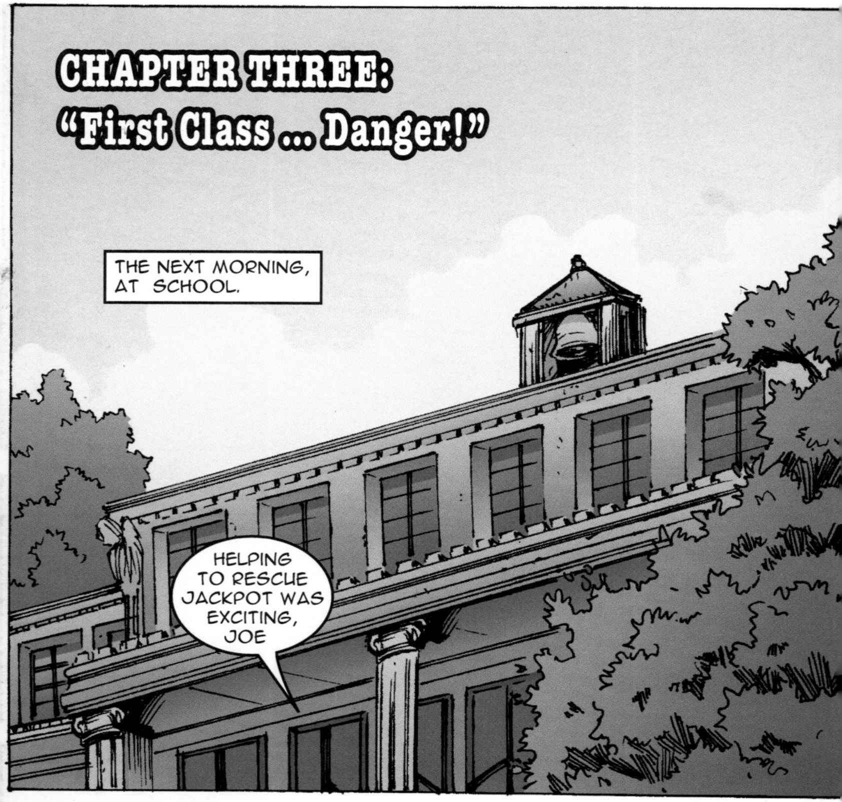
THE NEXT MORNING, AT SCHOOL.
HELPING TO RESCUE JACKPOT WAS EXCITING, JOE

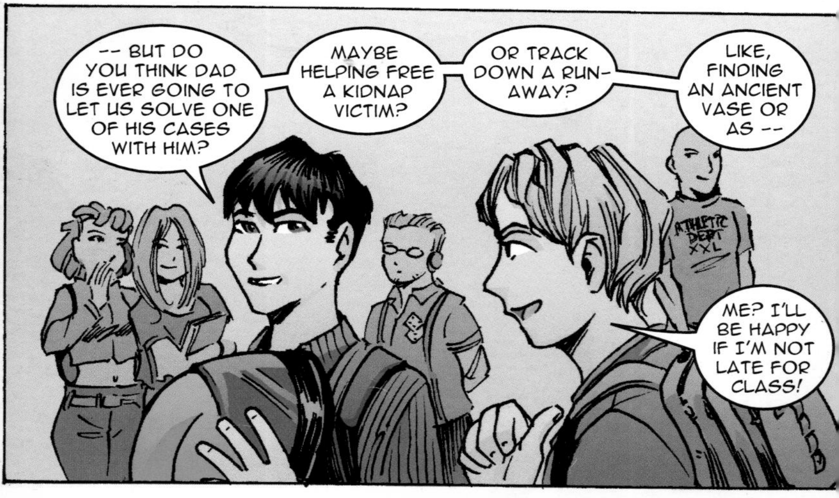
-- BUT DO YOU THINK DAD IS EVER GOING TO LET US SOLVE ONE OF HIS CASES WITH HIM?
MAYBE HELPING FREE A KIDNAP VICTIM?
OR TRACK DOWN A RUN-AWAY?
LIKE, FINDING AN ANCIENT VASE OR AS --
ATHLETIC DEPT XXL
ME? I'LL BE HAPPY IF I'M NOT LATE FOR CLASS!

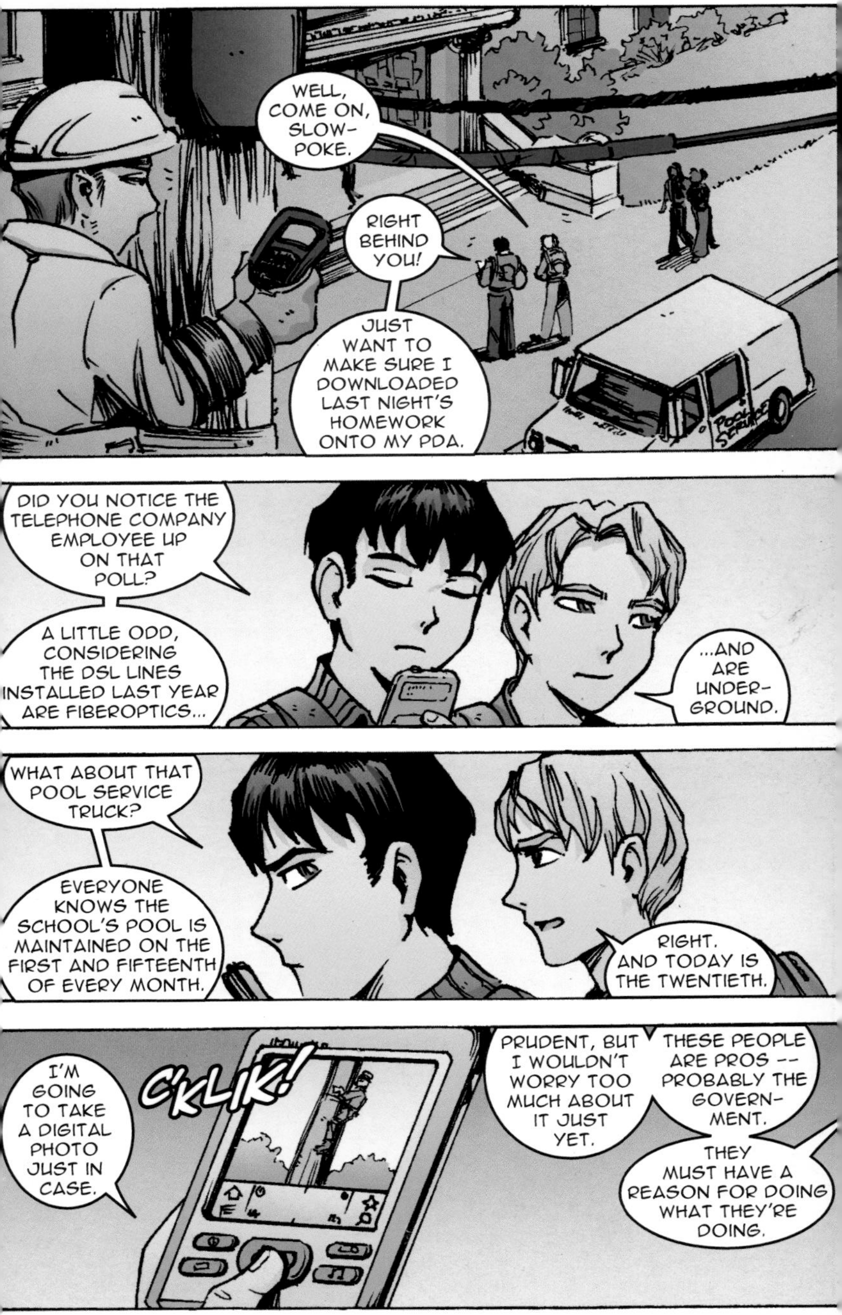
WELL, COME ON, SLOW-POKE.
RIGHT BEHIND YOU!
JUST WANT TO MAKE SURE I DOWNLOADED LAST NIGHT'S HOMEWORK ONTO MY PDA.
DID YOU NOTICE THE TELEPHONE COMPANY EMPLOYEE UP ON THAT POLL?
A LITTLE ODD, CONSIDERING THE DSL LINES INSTALLED LAST YEAR ARE FIBEROPTICS...
...AND ARE UNDER-GROUND.
WHAT ABOUT THAT POOL SERVICE TRUCK?
EVERYONE KNOWS THE SCHOOL'S POOL IS MAINTAINED ON THE FIRST AND FIFTEENTH OF EVERY MONTH.
RIGHT. AND TODAY IS THE TWENTIETH.
I'M GOING TO TAKE A DIGITAL PHOTO JUST IN CASE.
C'KLIK!
PRUDENT, BUT I WOULDN'T WORRY TOO MUCH ABOUT IT JUST YET.
THESE PEOPLE ARE PROS -- PROBABLY THE GOVERN-MENT.
THEY MUST HAVE A REASON FOR DOING WHAT THEY'RE DOING.

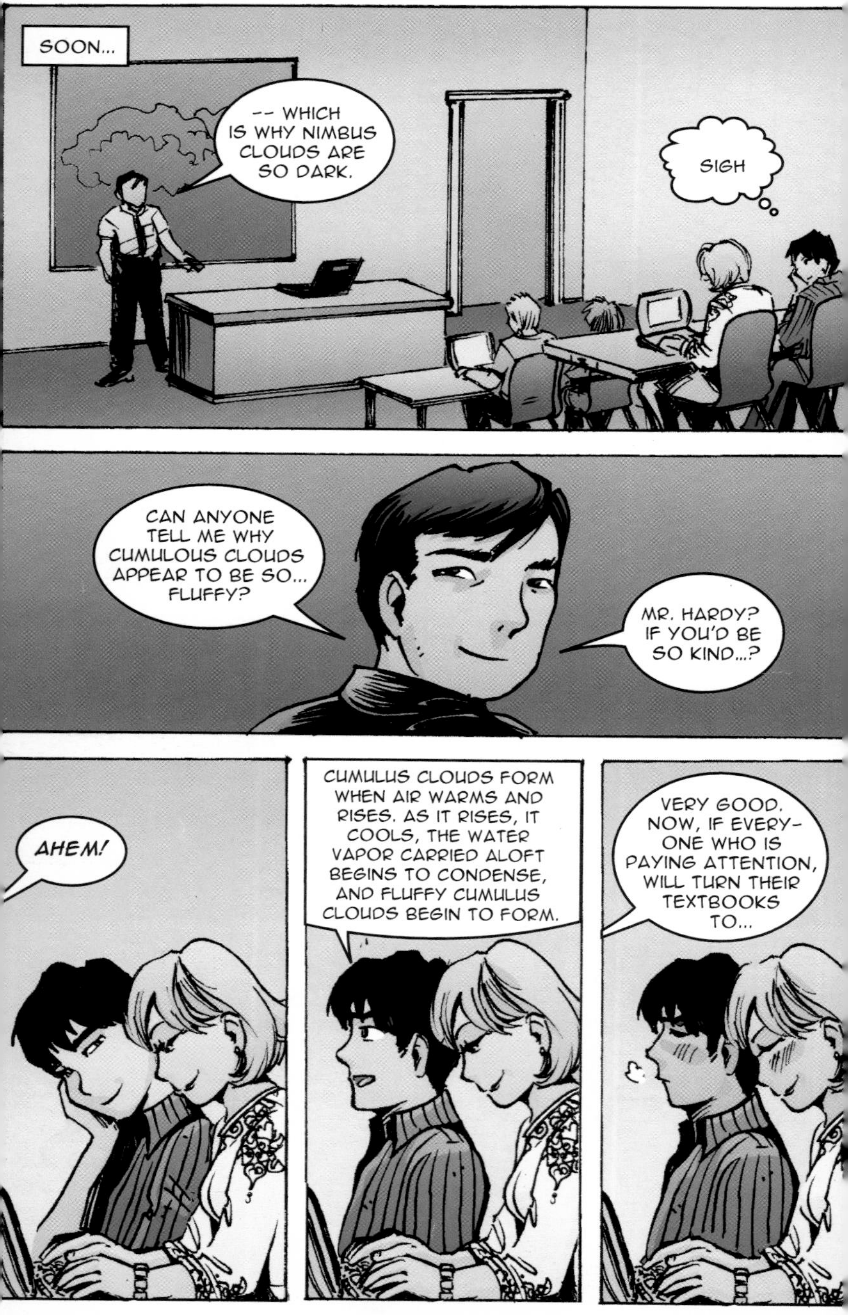
SOON...
-- WHICH IS WHY NIMBUS CLOUDS ARE SO DARK.
SIGH
CAN ANYONE TELL ME WHY CUMULOUS CLOUDS APPEAR TO BE SO... FLUFFY?
MR. HARDY? IF YOU'D BE SO KIND...?
AHEM!
CUMULUS CLOUDS FORM WHEN AIR WARMS AND RISES. AS IT RISES, IT COOLS, THE WATER VAPOR CARRIED ALOFT BEGINS TO CONDENSE, AND FLUFFY CUMULUS CLOUDS BEGIN TO FORM.
VERY GOOD. NOW, IF EVERY-ONE WHO IS PAYING ATTENTION, WILL TURN THEIR TEXTBOOKS TO...

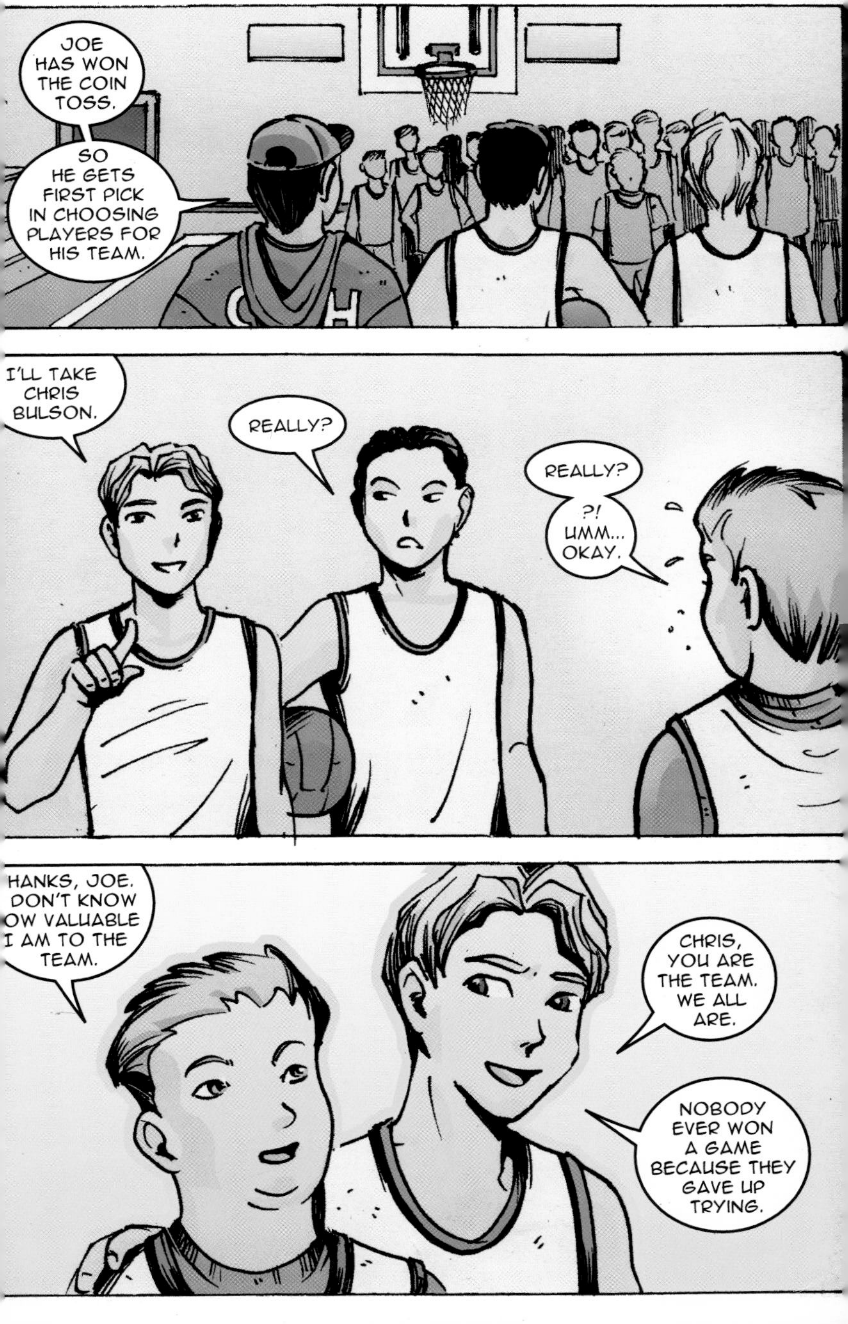

JOE HAS WON THE COIN TOSS.
SO HE GETS FIRST PICK IN CHOOSING PLAYERS FOR HIS TEAM.
I'LL TAKE CHRIS BULSON.
REALLY?
REALLY?
?! UMM... OKAY.
HANKS, JOE. DON'T KNOW OW VALUABLE I AM TO THE TEAM.
CHRIS, YOU ARE THE TEAM. WE ALL ARE.
NOBODY EVER WON A GAME BECAUSE THEY GAVE UP TRYING.

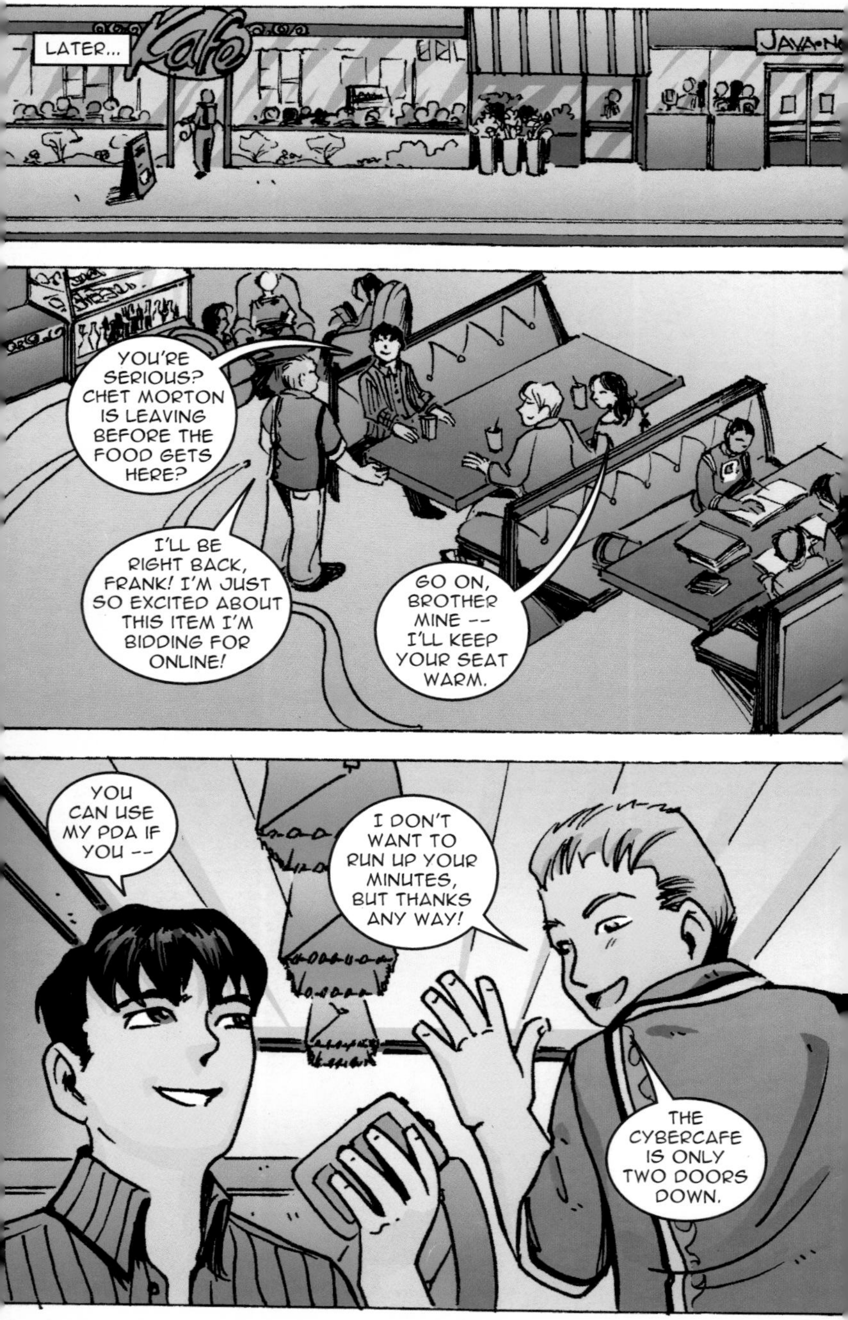
LATER...
KAFE
JAVA•N
YOU'RE SERIOUS? CHET MORTON IS LEAVING BEFORE THE FOOD GETS HERE?
I'LL BE RIGHT BACK, FRANK! I'M JUST SO EXCITED ABOUT THIS ITEM I'M BIDDING FOR ONLINE!
GO ON, BROTHER MINE -- I'LL KEEP YOUR SEAT WARM.
YOU CAN USE MY PDA IF YOU --
I DON'T WANT TO RUN UP YOUR MINUTES, BUT THANKS ANY WAY!
THE CYBERCAFE IS ONLY TWO DOORS DOWN.

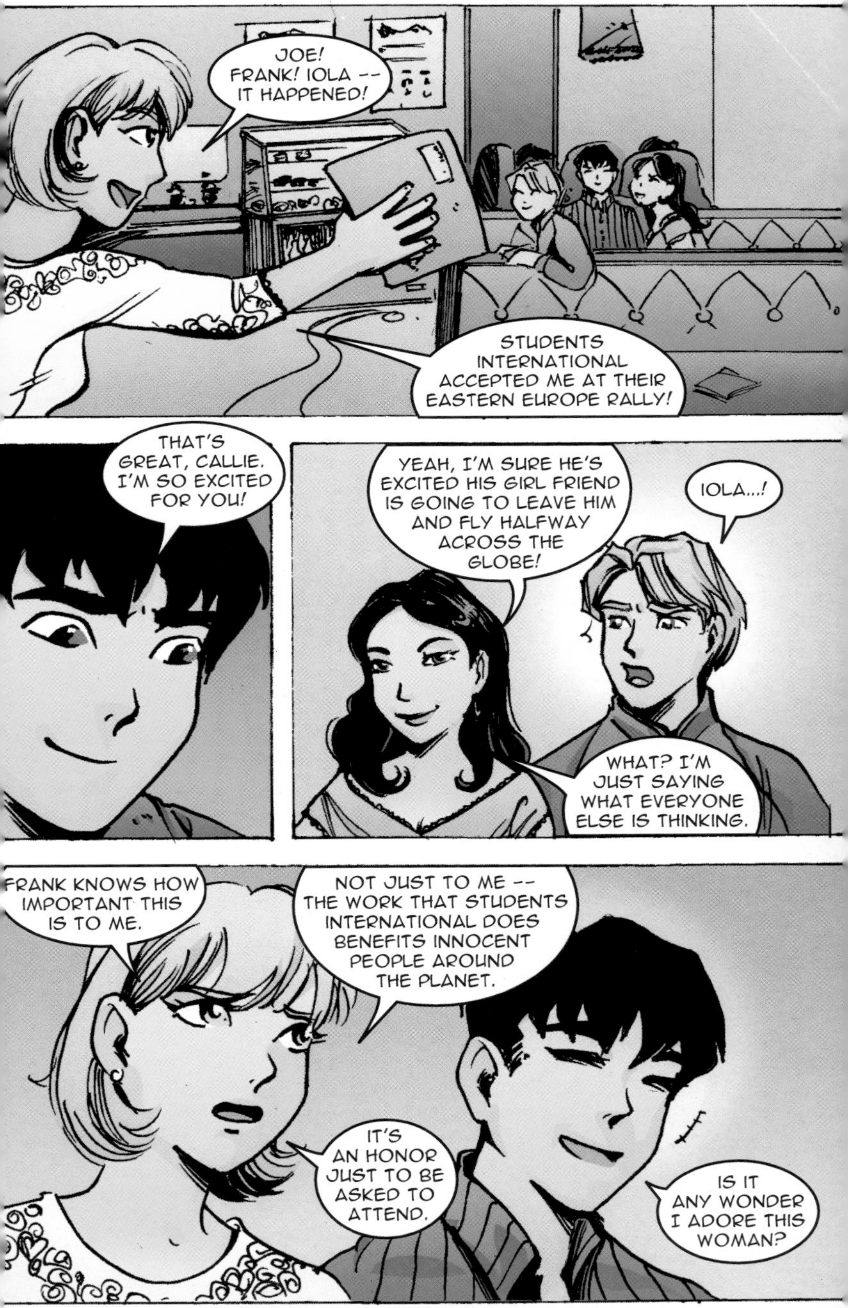
JOE! FRANK! IOLA -- IT HAPPENED!
STUDENTS INTERNATIONAL ACCEPTED ME AT THEIR EASTERN EUROPE RALLY!
THAT'S GREAT, CALLIE. I'M SO EXCITED FOR YOU!
YEAH, I'M SURE HE'S EXCITED HIS GIRL FRIEND IS GOING TO LEAVE HIM AND FLY HALFWAY ACROSS THE GLOBE!
IOLA...!
WHAT? I'M JUST SAYING WHAT EVERYONE ELSE IS THINKING.
FRANK KNOWS HOW IMPORTANT THIS IS TO ME.
NOT JUST TO ME -- THE WORK THAT STUDENTS INTERNATIONAL DOES BENEFITS INNOCENT PEOPLE AROUND THE PLANET.
IT'S AN HONOR JUST TO BE ASKED TO ATTEND.
IS IT ANY WONDER I ADORE THIS WOMAN?

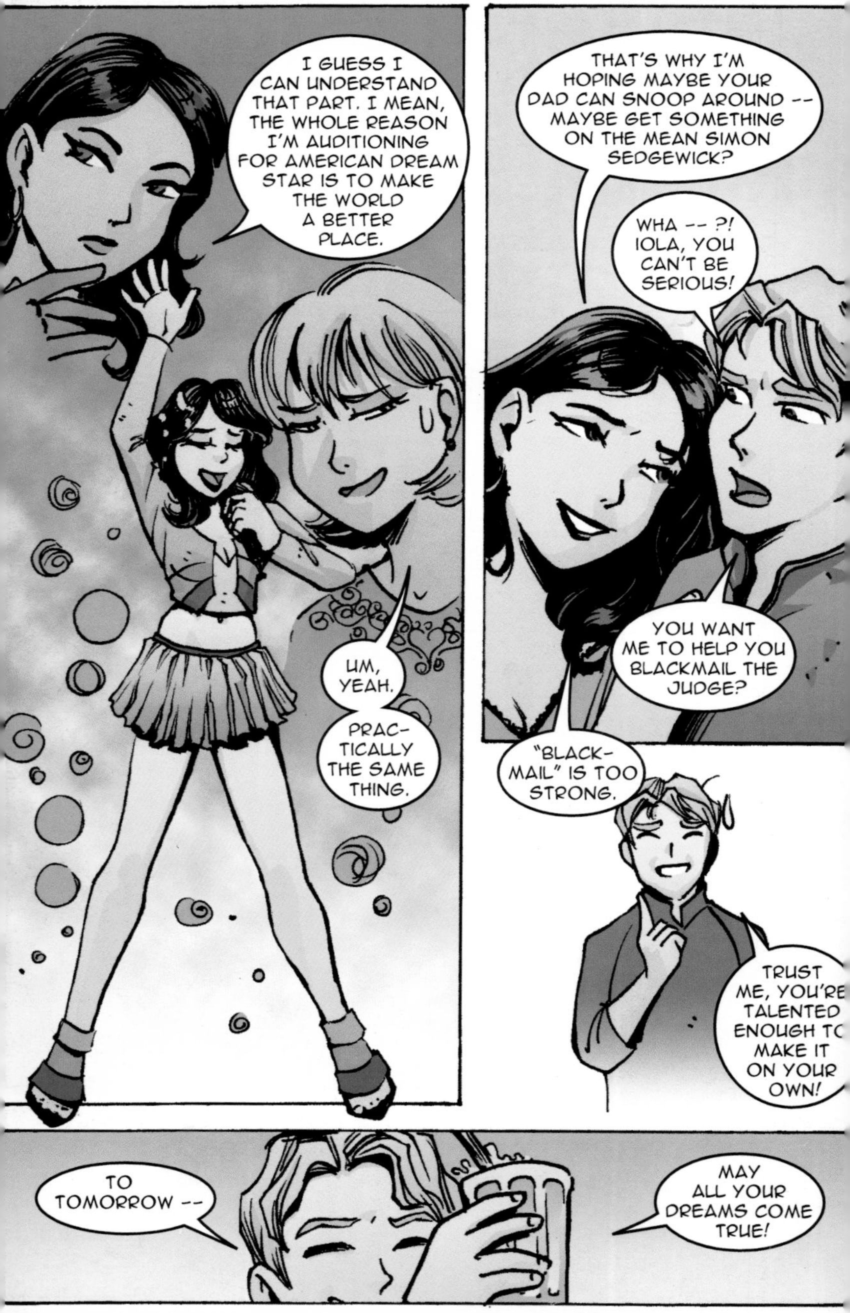
I GUESS I CAN UNDERSTAND THAT PART. I MEAN, THE WHOLE REASON I'M AUDITIONING FOR AMERICAN DREAM STAR IS TO MAKE THE WORLD A BETTER PLACE.
UM, YEAH.
PRAC-TICALLY THE SAME THING.
THAT'S WHY I'M HOPING MAYBE YOUR DAD CAN SNOOP AROUND -- MAYBE GET SOMETHING ON THE MEAN SIMON SEDGEWICK?
WHA -- ?! IOLA, YOU CAN'T BE SERIOUS!
YOU WANT ME TO HELP YOU BLACKMAIL THE JUDGE?
"BLACK-MAIL" IS TOO STRONG.
TRUST ME, YOU'RE TALENTED ENOUGH TO MAKE IT ON YOUR OWN!
TO TOMORROW --
MAY ALL YOUR DREAMS COME TRUE!

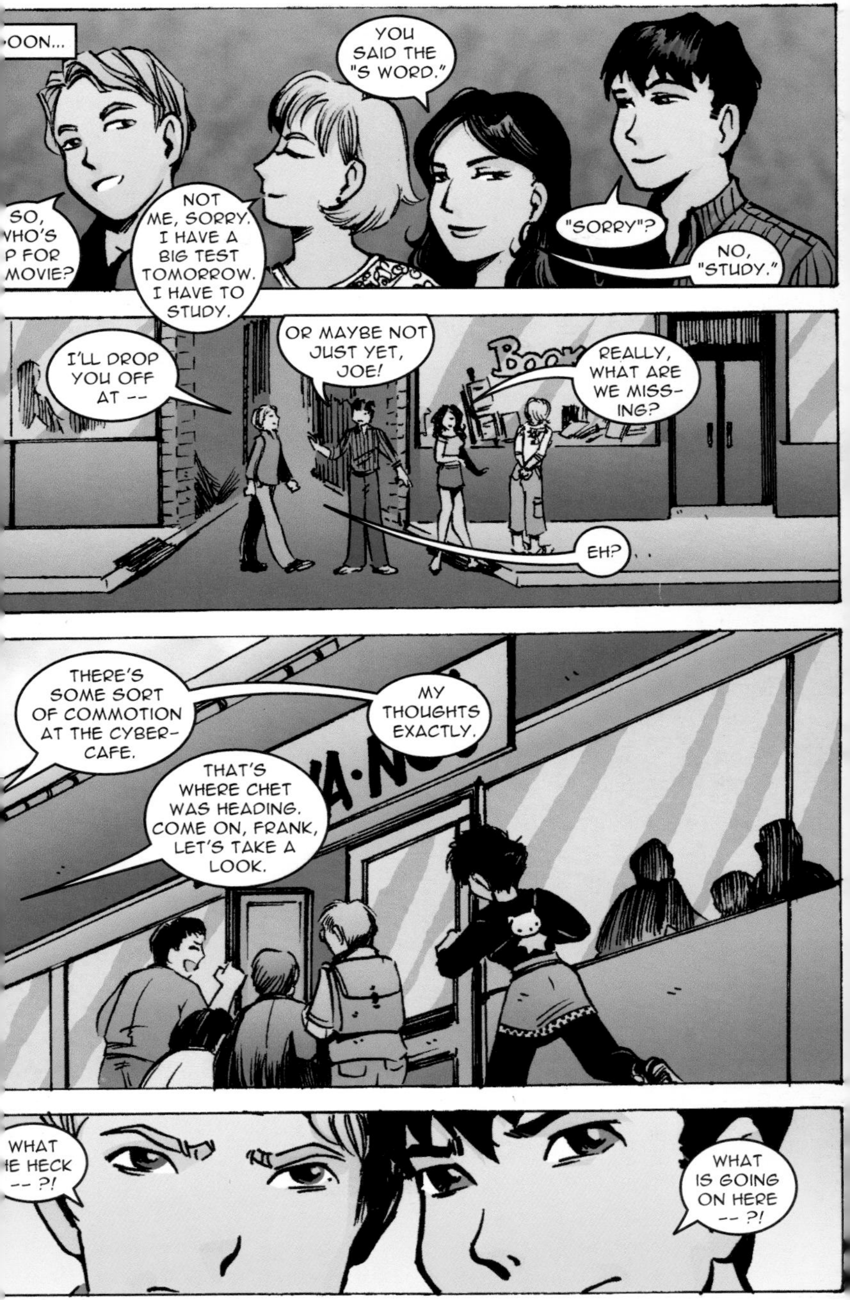
OON...
SO, WHO'S P FOR MOVIE?
NOT ME, SORRY. I HAVE A BIG TEST TOMORROW. I HAVE TO STUDY.
YOU SAID THE "S WORD."
"SORRY"?
NO, "STUDY."
I'LL DROP YOU OFF AT --
OR MAYBE NOT JUST YET, JOE!
REALLY, WHAT ARE WE MISSING?
EH?
THERE'S SOME SORT OF COMMOTION AT THE CYBER-CAFE.
MY THOUGHTS EXACTLY.
THAT'S WHERE CHET WAS HEADING. COME ON, FRANK, LET'S TAKE A LOOK.
WHAT IE HECK -- ?!
WHAT IS GOING ON HERE -- ?!

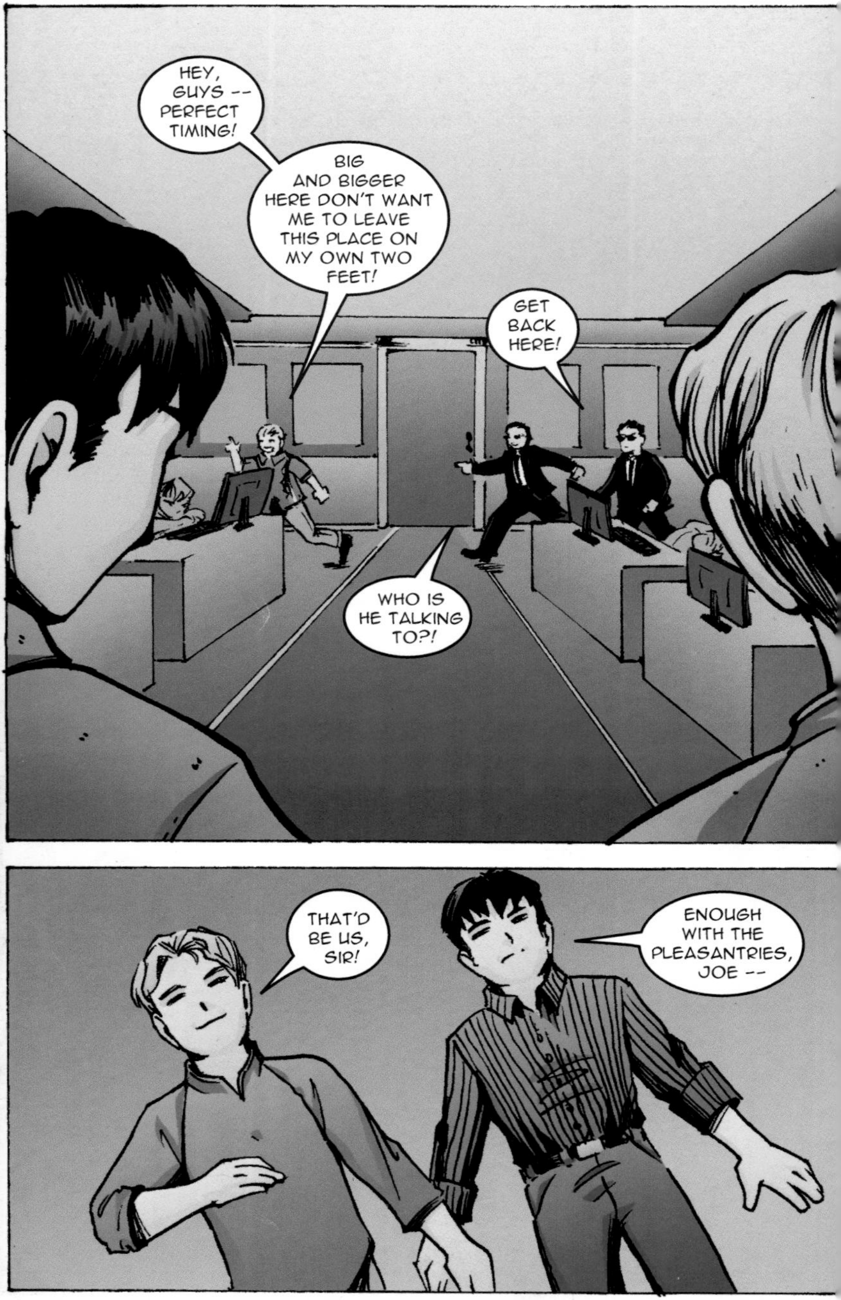
HEY, GUYS -- PERFECT TIMING!
BIG AND BIGGER HERE DON'T WANT ME TO LEAVE THIS PLACE ON MY OWN TWO FEET!
GET BACK HERE!
WHO IS HE TALKING TO?!
THAT'D BE US, SIR!
ENOUGH WITH THE PLEASANTRIES, JOE --

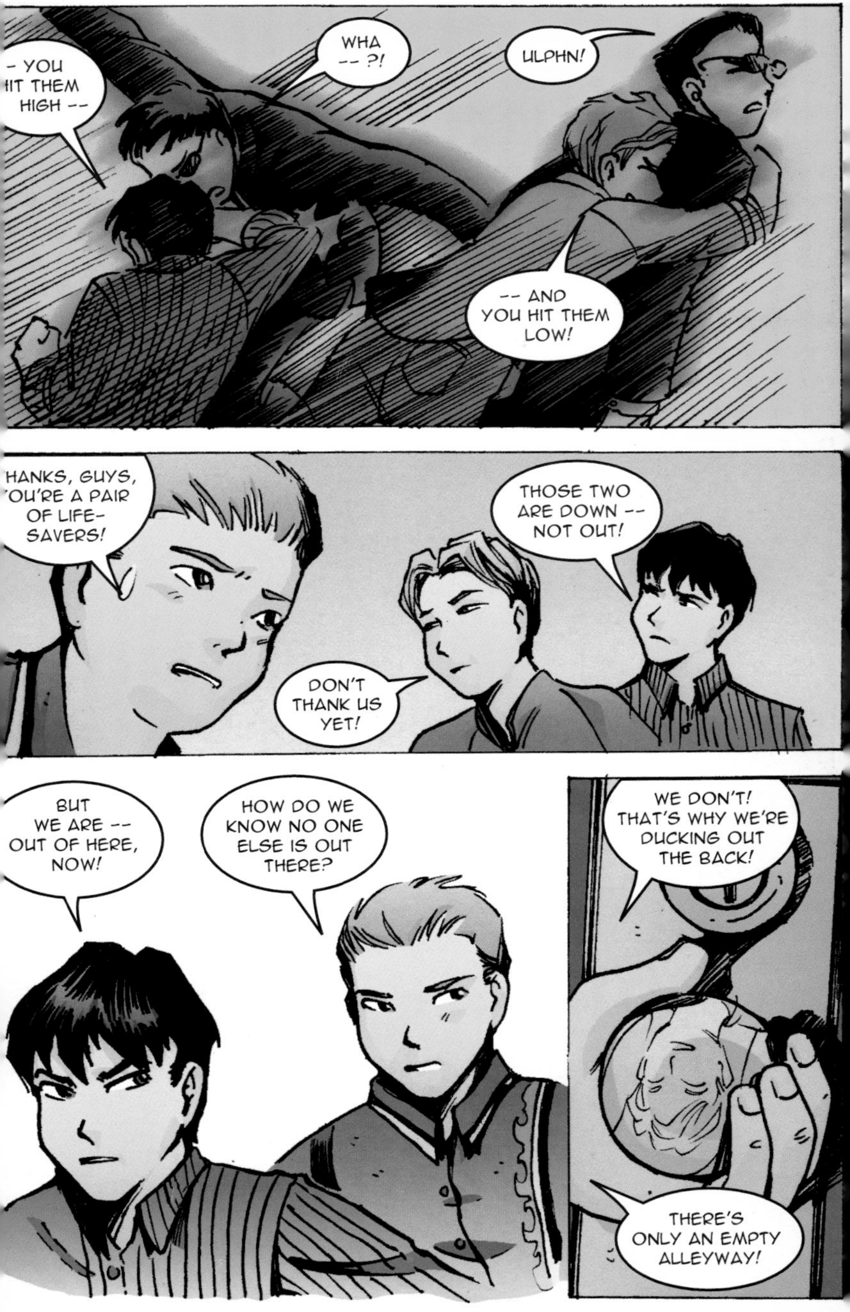
- YOU
HIT THEM
HIGH --
WHA
-- ?!
ULPHN!
-- AND
YOU HIT THEM
LOW!
HANKS, GUYS,
OU'RE A PAIR
OF LIFE-
SAVERS!
THOSE TWO
ARE DOWN --
NOT OUT!
DON'T
THANK US
YET!
BUT
WE ARE --
OUT OF HERE,
NOW!
HOW DO WE
KNOW NO ONE
ELSE IS OUT
THERE?
WE DON'T!
THAT'S WHY WE'RE
DUCKING OUT
THE BACK!
THERE'S
ONLY AN EMPTY
ALLEYWAY!

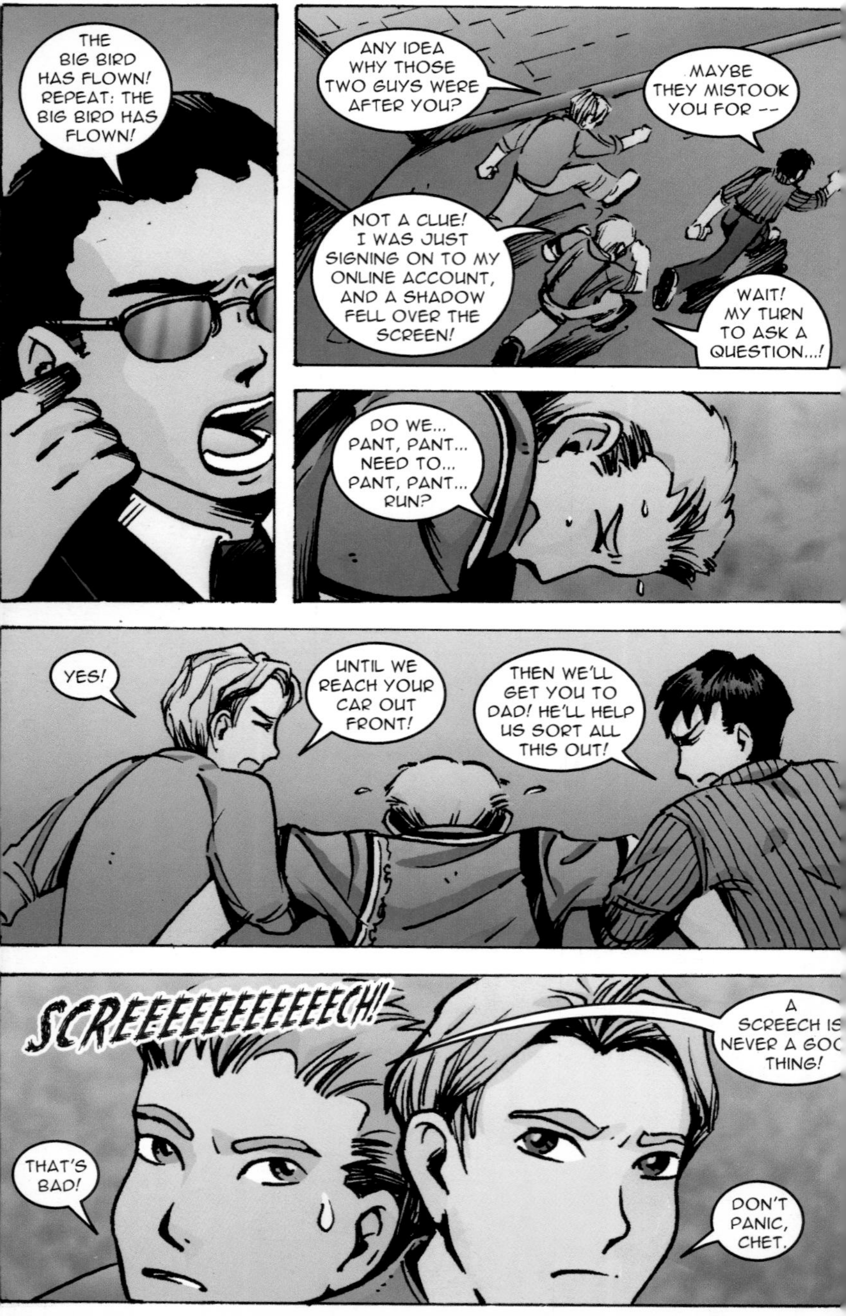
THE BIG BIRD HAS FLOWN! REPEAT: THE BIG BIRD HAS FLOWN!
ANY IDEA WHY THOSE TWO GUYS WERE AFTER YOU?
MAYBE THEY MISTOOK YOU FOR --
NOT A CLUE! I WAS JUST SIGNING ON TO MY ONLINE ACCOUNT, AND A SHADOW FELL OVER THE SCREEN!
WAIT! MY TURN TO ASK A QUESTION...!
DO WE... PANT, PANT... NEED TO... PANT, PANT... RUN?
YES!
UNTIL WE REACH YOUR CAR OUT FRONT!
THEN WE'LL GET YOU TO DAD! HE'LL HELP US SORT ALL THIS OUT!
SCREEEEEEEEEEEEECH!
A SCREECH IS NEVER A GOO THING!
THAT'S BAD!
DON'T PANIC, CHET.

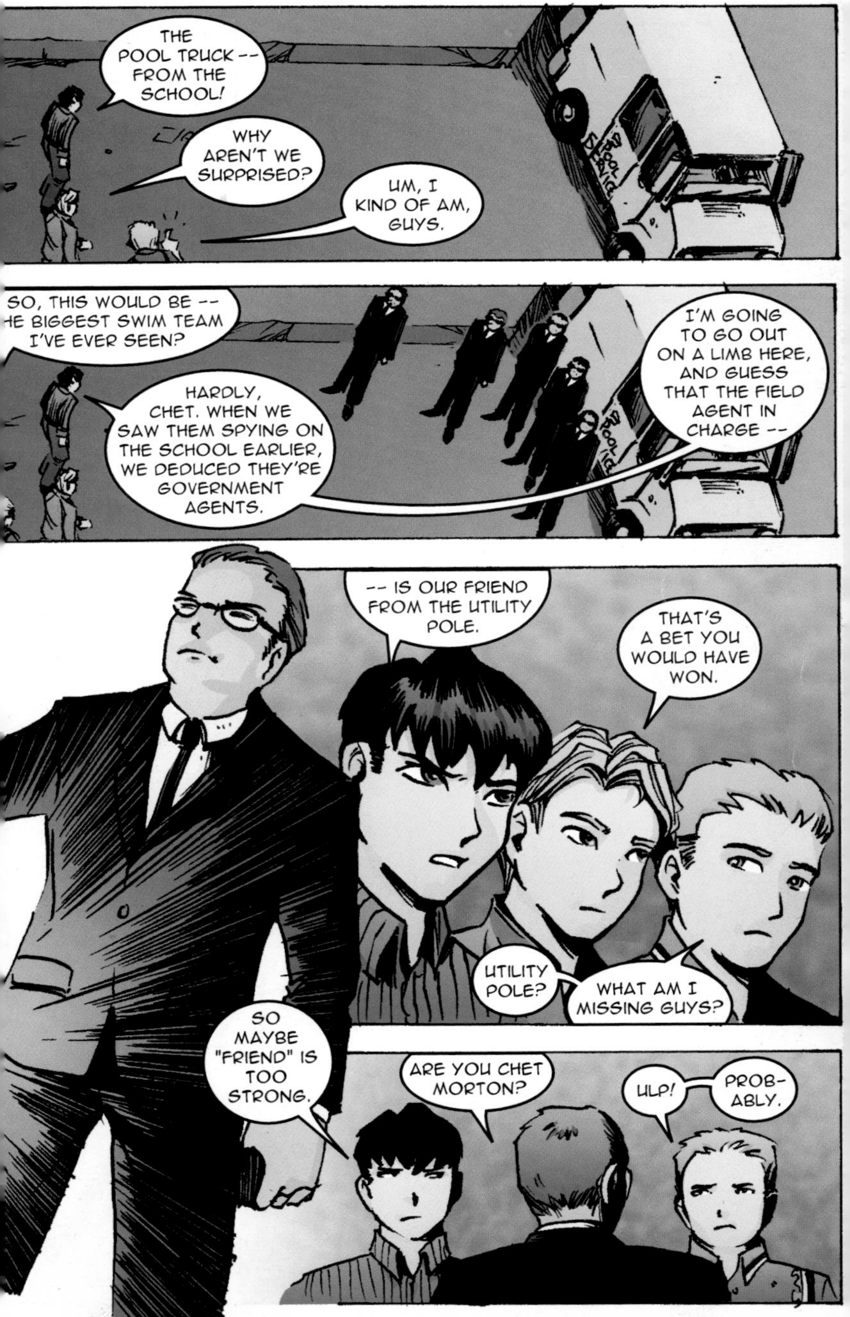
THE POOL TRUCK -- FROM THE SCHOOL!
WHY AREN'T WE SURPRISED?
UM, I KIND OF AM, GUYS.
SO, THIS WOULD BE -- HE BIGGEST SWIM TEAM I'VE EVER SEEN?
HARDLY, CHET. WHEN WE SAW THEM SPYING ON THE SCHOOL EARLIER, WE DEDUCED THEY'RE GOVERNMENT AGENTS.
I'M GOING TO GO OUT ON A LIMB HERE, AND GUESS THAT THE FIELD AGENT IN CHARGE --
-- IS OUR FRIEND FROM THE UTILITY POLE.
THAT'S A BET YOU WOULD HAVE WON.
UTILITY POLE?
WHAT AM I MISSING GUYS?
SO MAYBE "FRIEND" IS TOO STRONG.
ARE YOU CHET MORTON?
ULP!
PROB-ABLY.

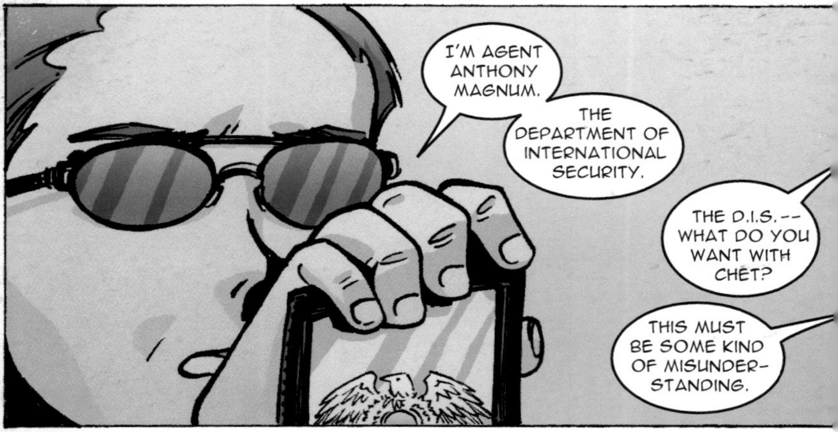
I'M AGENT ANTHONY MAGNUM.
THE DEPARTMENT OF INTERNATIONAL SECURITY.
THE D.I.S. -- WHAT DO YOU WANT WITH CHET?
THIS MUST BE SOME KIND OF MISUNDER-STANDING.

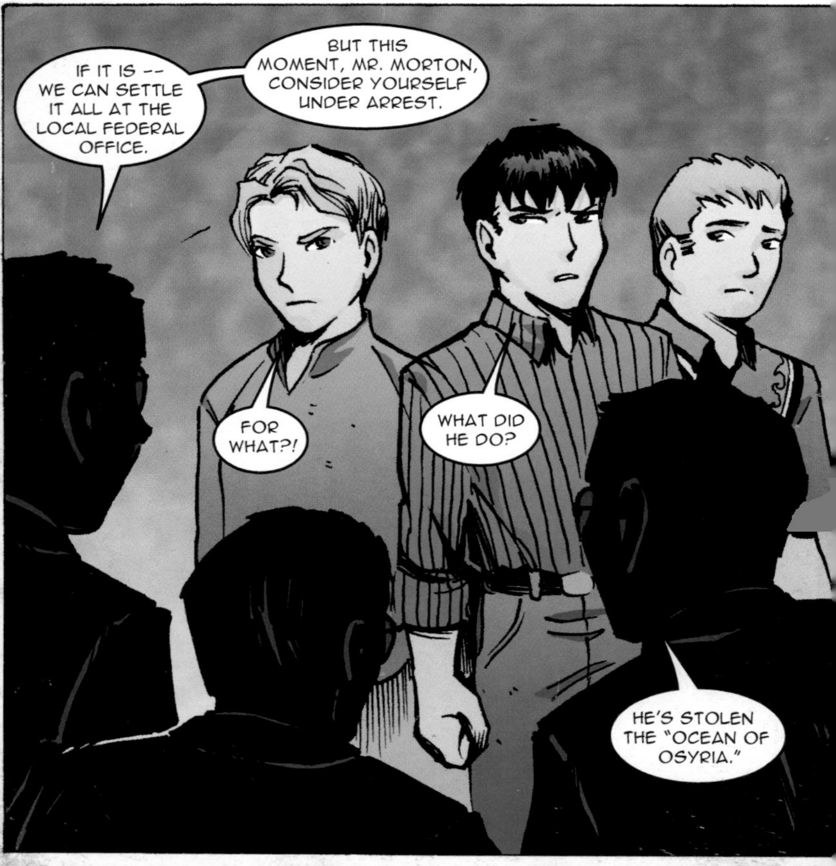
IF IT IS -- WE CAN SETTLE IT ALL AT THE LOCAL FEDERAL OFFICE.
BUT THIS MOMENT, MR. MORTON, CONSIDER YOURSELF UNDER ARREST.
FOR WHAT?!
WHAT DID HE DO?
HE'S STOLEN THE "OCEAN OF OSYRIA."

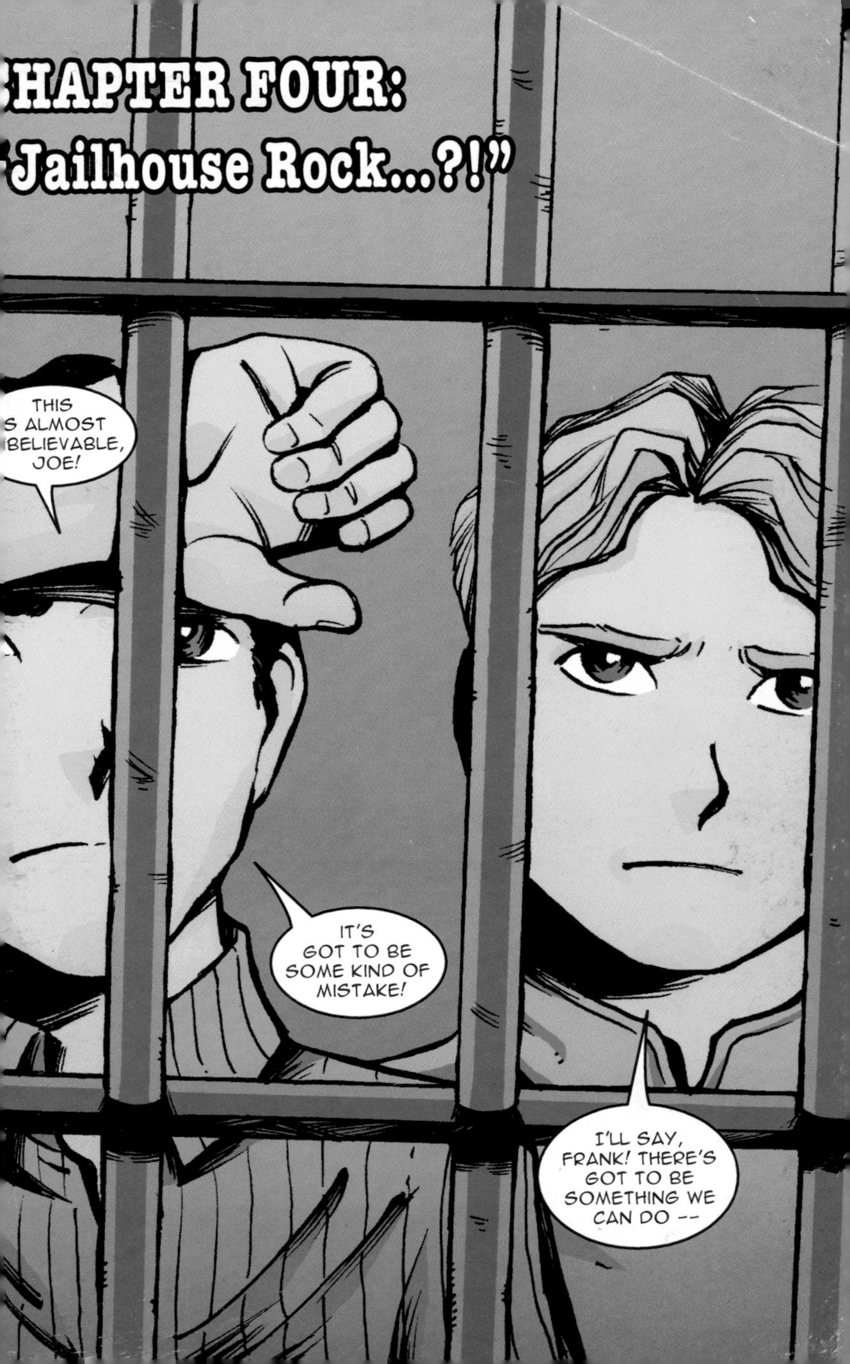
HAPTER FOUR:
'Jailhouse Rock...?!"
THIS S ALMOST BELIEVABLE, JOE!
IT'S GOT TO BE SOME KIND OF MISTAKE!
I'LL SAY, FRANK! THERE'S GOT TO BE SOMETHING WE CAN DO --

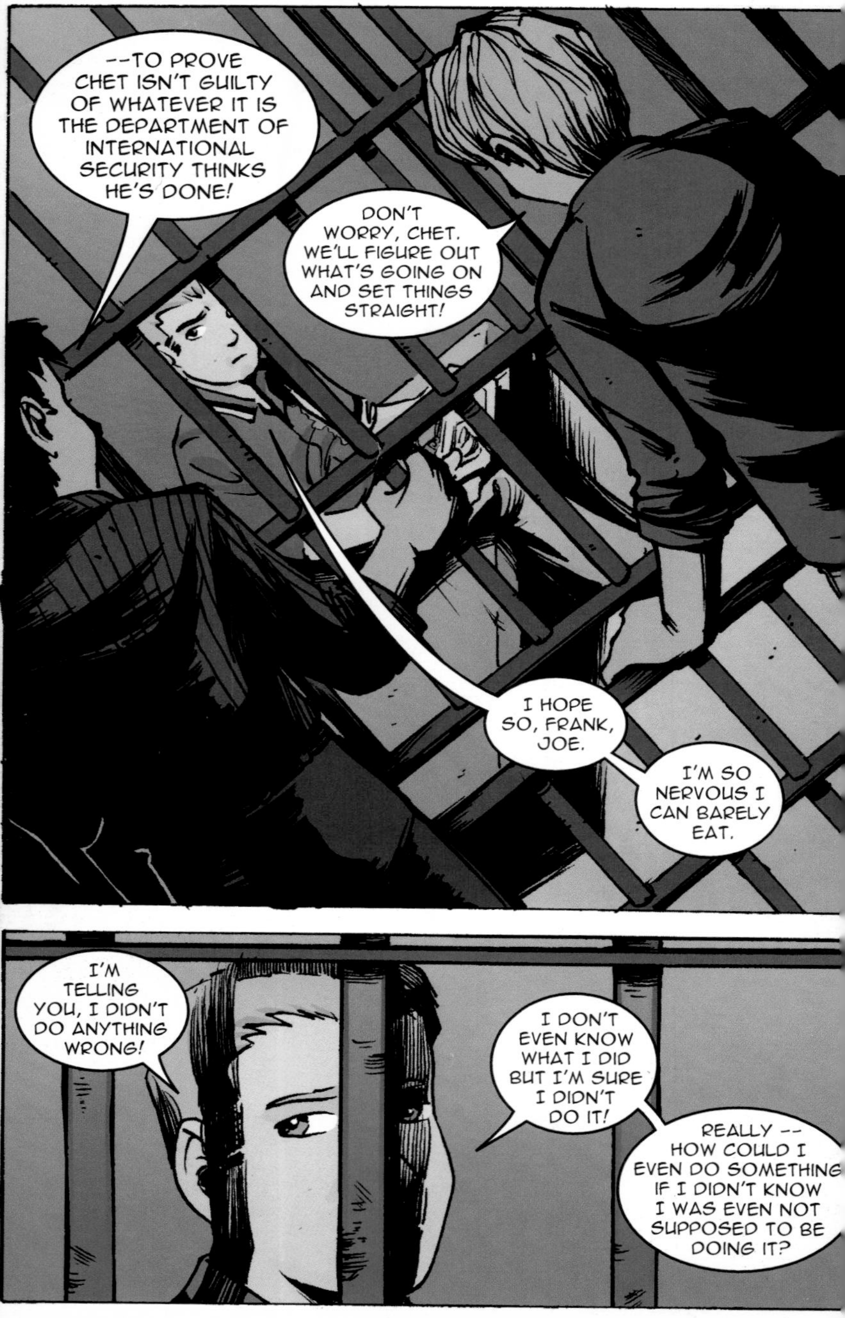
--TO PROVE CHET ISN'T GUILTY OF WHATEVER IT IS THE DEPARTMENT OF INTERNATIONAL SECURITY THINKS HE'S DONE!
DON'T WORRY, CHET. WE'LL FIGURE OUT WHAT'S GOING ON AND SET THINGS STRAIGHT!
I HOPE SO, FRANK, JOE.
I'M SO NERVOUS I CAN BARELY EAT.
I'M TELLING YOU, I DIDN'T DO ANYTHING WRONG!
I DON'T EVEN KNOW WHAT I DID BUT I'M SURE I DIDN'T DO IT!
REALLY -- HOW COULD I EVEN DO SOMETHING IF I DIDN'T KNOW I WAS EVEN NOT SUPPOSED TO BE DOING IT?

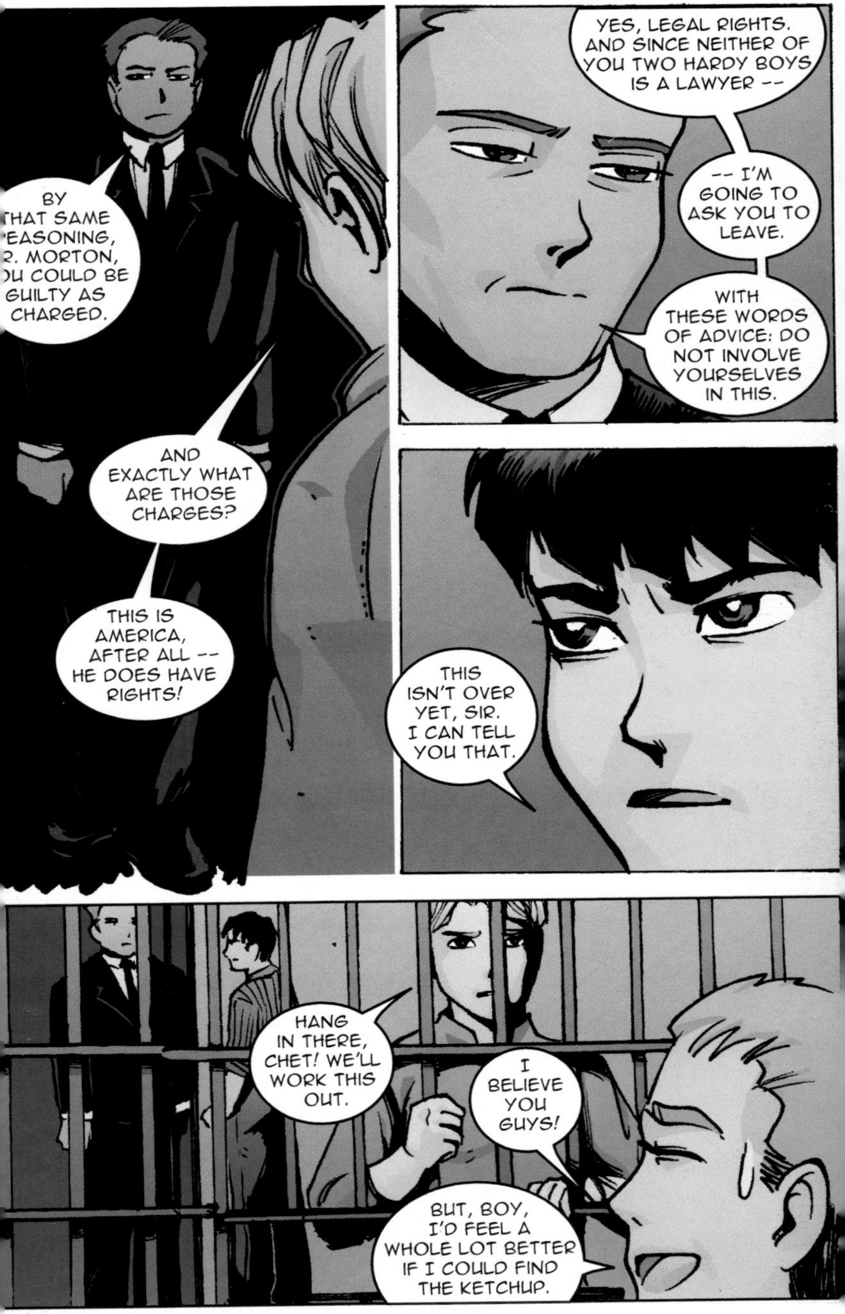

BY THAT SAME EASONING, R. MORTON, OU COULD BE GUILTY AS CHARGED.
AND EXACTLY WHAT ARE THOSE CHARGES?
THIS IS AMERICA, AFTER ALL -- HE DOES HAVE RIGHTS!
YES, LEGAL RIGHTS. AND SINCE NEITHER OF YOU TWO HARDY BOYS IS A LAWYER --
-- I'M GOING TO ASK YOU TO LEAVE.
WITH THESE WORDS OF ADVICE: DO NOT INVOLVE YOURSELVES IN THIS.
THIS ISN'T OVER YET, SIR. I CAN TELL YOU THAT.
HANG IN THERE, CHET! WE'LL WORK THIS OUT.
I BELIEVE YOU GUYS!
BUT, BOY, I'D FEEL A WHOLE LOT BETTER IF I COULD FIND THE KETCHUP.

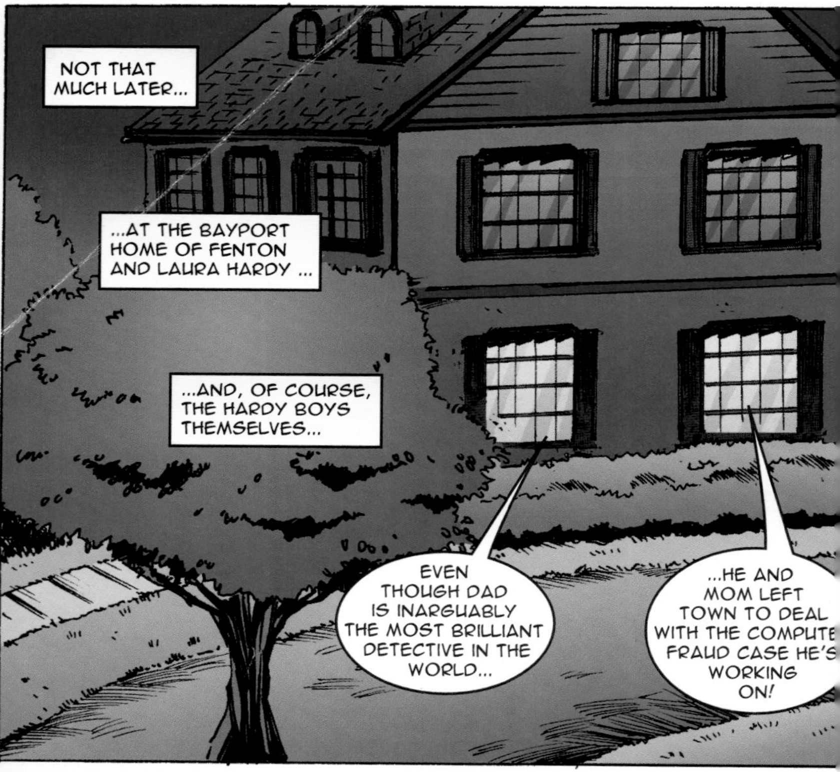
NOT THAT MUCH LATER...
...AT THE BAYPORT HOME OF FENTON AND LAURA HARDY ...
...AND, OF COURSE, THE HARDY BOYS THEMSELVES...
EVEN THOUGH DAD IS INARGUABLY THE MOST BRILLIANT DETECTIVE IN THE WORLD...
...HE AND MOM LEFT TOWN TO DEAL WITH THE COMPUTE FRAUD CASE HE'S WORKING ON!

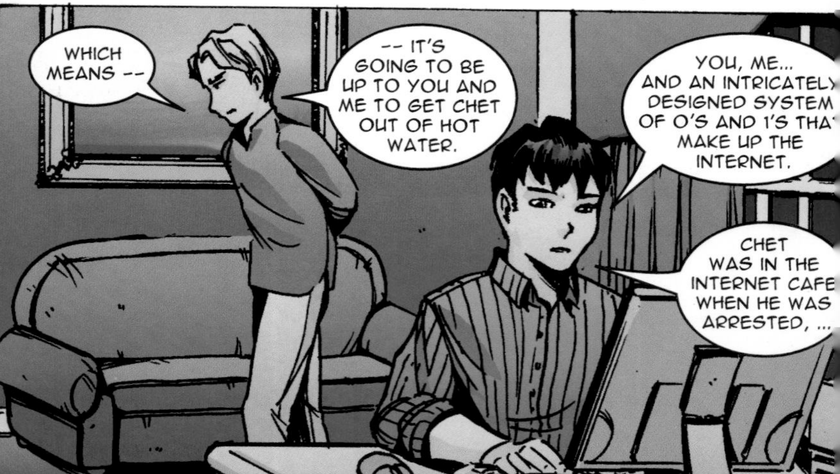
WHICH MEANS --
-- IT'S GOING TO BE UP TO YOU AND ME TO GET CHET OUT OF HOT WATER.
YOU, ME... AND AN INTRICATEL DESIGNED SYSTEM OF 0'S AND 1'S THA MAKE UP THE INTERNET.
CHET WAS IN THE INTERNET CAFE WHEN HE WAS ARRESTED, ...

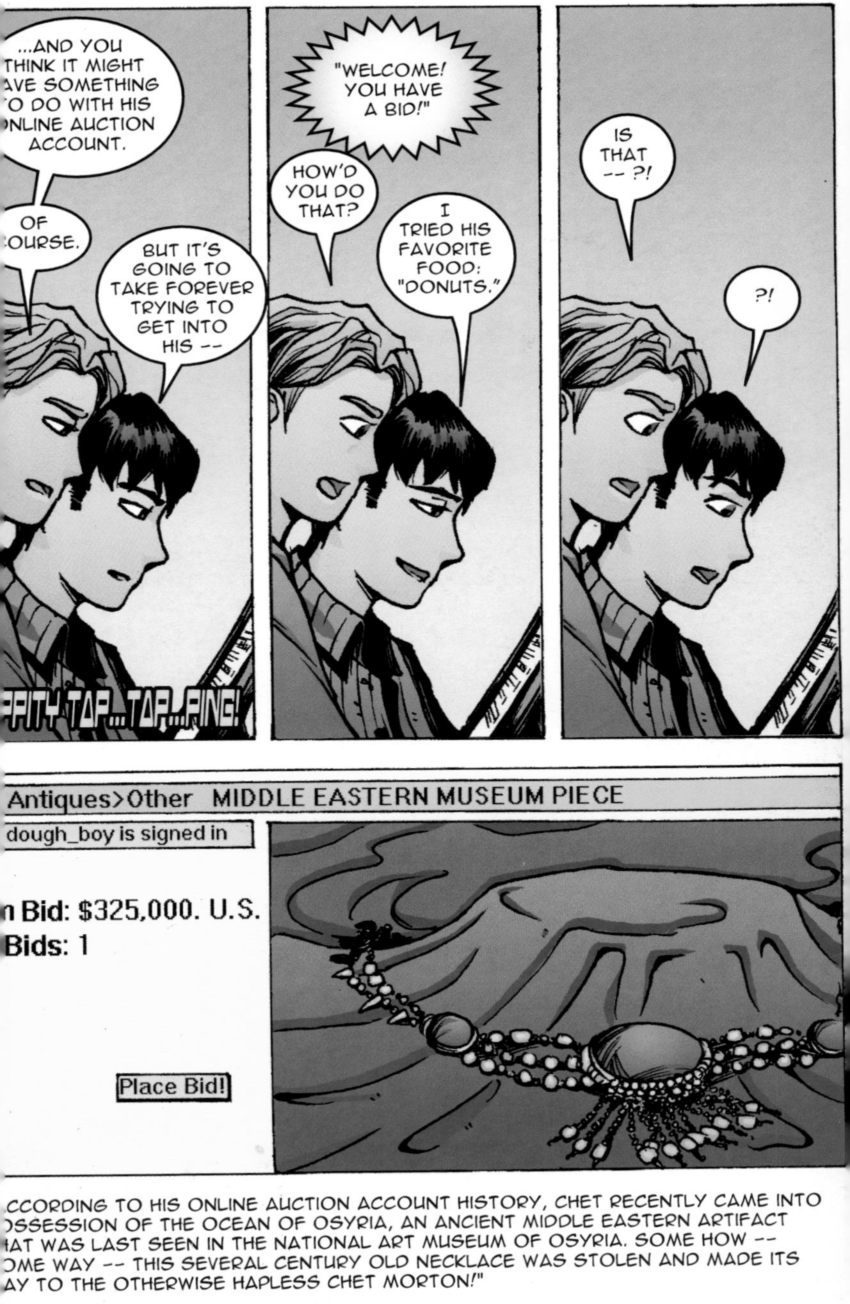

...AND YOU THINK IT MIGHT AVE SOMETHING TO DO WITH HIS ONLINE AUCTION ACCOUNT.
OF COURSE.
BUT IT'S GOING TO TAKE FOREVER TRYING TO GET INTO HIS --
PFITY TAP...TAP...PING!
"WELCOME! YOU HAVE A BID!"
HOW'D YOU DO THAT?
I TRIED HIS FAVORITE FOOD: "DONUTS."
IS THAT -- ?!
?!
Antiques>Other MIDDLE EASTERN MUSEUM PIECE
dough_boy is signed in
n Bid: $325,000. U.S.
Bids: 1
Place Bid!
CCORDING TO HIS ONLINE AUCTION ACCOUNT HISTORY, CHET RECENTLY CAME INTO OSSESSION OF THE OCEAN OF OSYRIA, AN ANCIENT MIDDLE EASTERN ARTIFACT HAT WAS LAST SEEN IN THE NATIONAL ART MUSEUM OF OSYRIA. SOME HOW -- OME WAY -- THIS SEVERAL CENTURY OLD NECKLACE WAS STOLEN AND MADE ITS AY TO THE OTHERWISE HAPLESS CHET MORTON!"

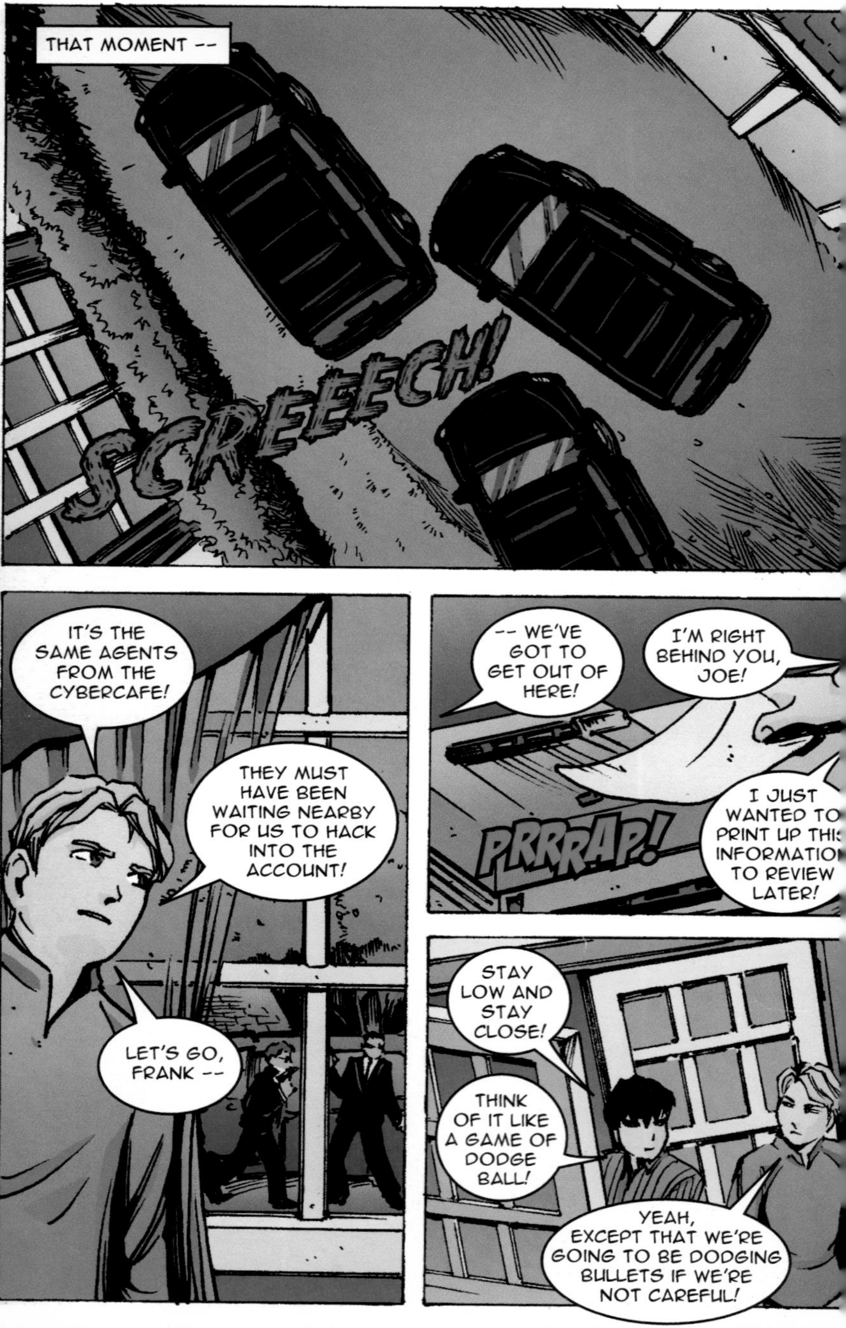
THAT MOMENT --
SCREEECH!
IT'S THE SAME AGENTS FROM THE CYBERCAFE!
THEY MUST HAVE BEEN WAITING NEARBY FOR US TO HACK INTO THE ACCOUNT!
LET'S GO, FRANK --
-- WE'VE GOT TO GET OUT OF HERE!
I'M RIGHT BEHIND YOU, JOE!
PRRRAP!
I JUST WANTED TO PRINT UP THIS INFORMATION TO REVIEW LATER!
STAY LOW AND STAY CLOSE!
THINK OF IT LIKE A GAME OF DODGE BALL!
YEAH, EXCEPT THAT WE'RE GOING TO BE DODGING BULLETS IF WE'RE NOT CAREFUL!

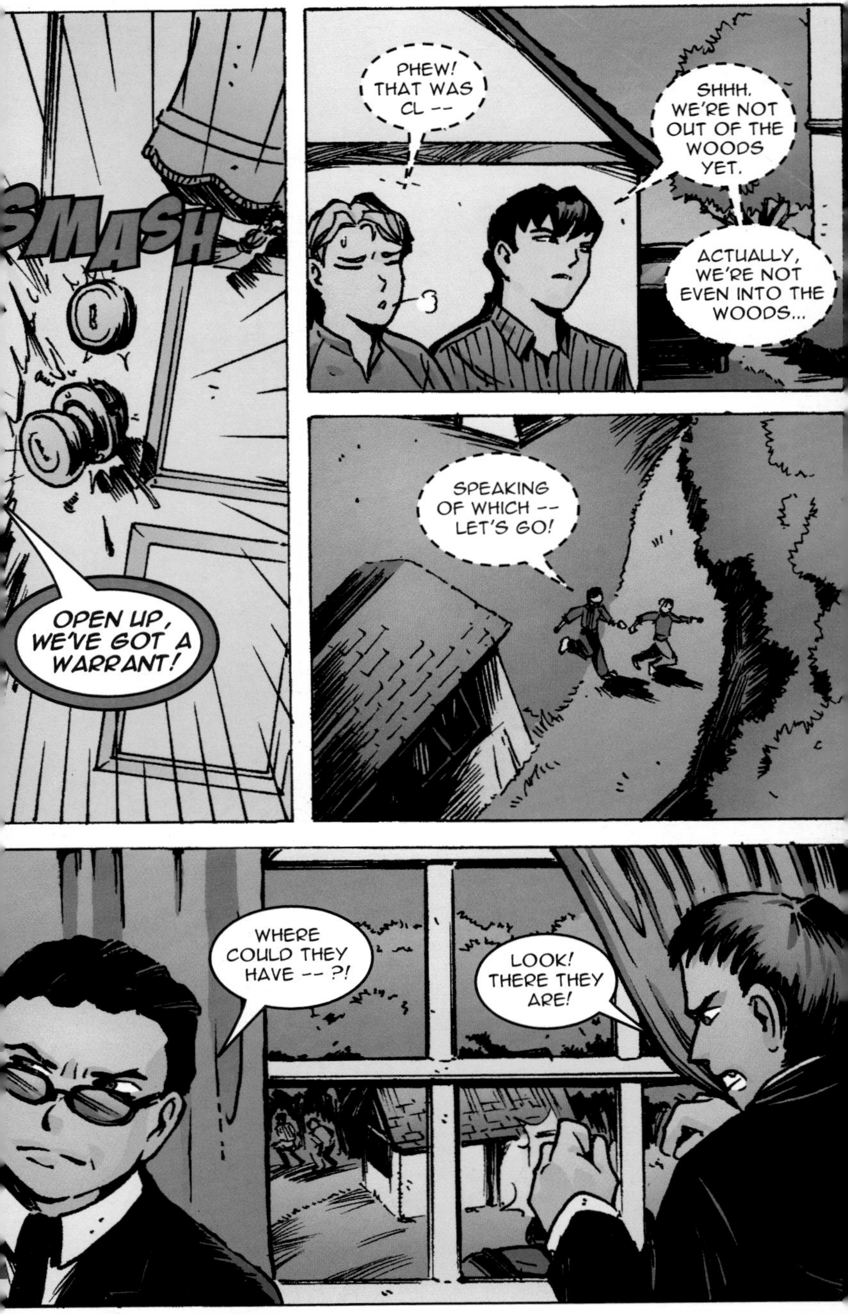
SMASH
OPEN UP, WE'VE GOT A WARRANT!
PHEW! THAT WAS CL --
SHHH. WE'RE NOT OUT OF THE WOODS YET.
ACTUALLY, WE'RE NOT EVEN INTO THE WOODS...
SPEAKING OF WHICH -- LET'S GO!
WHERE COULD THEY HAVE -- ?!
LOOK! THERE THEY ARE!

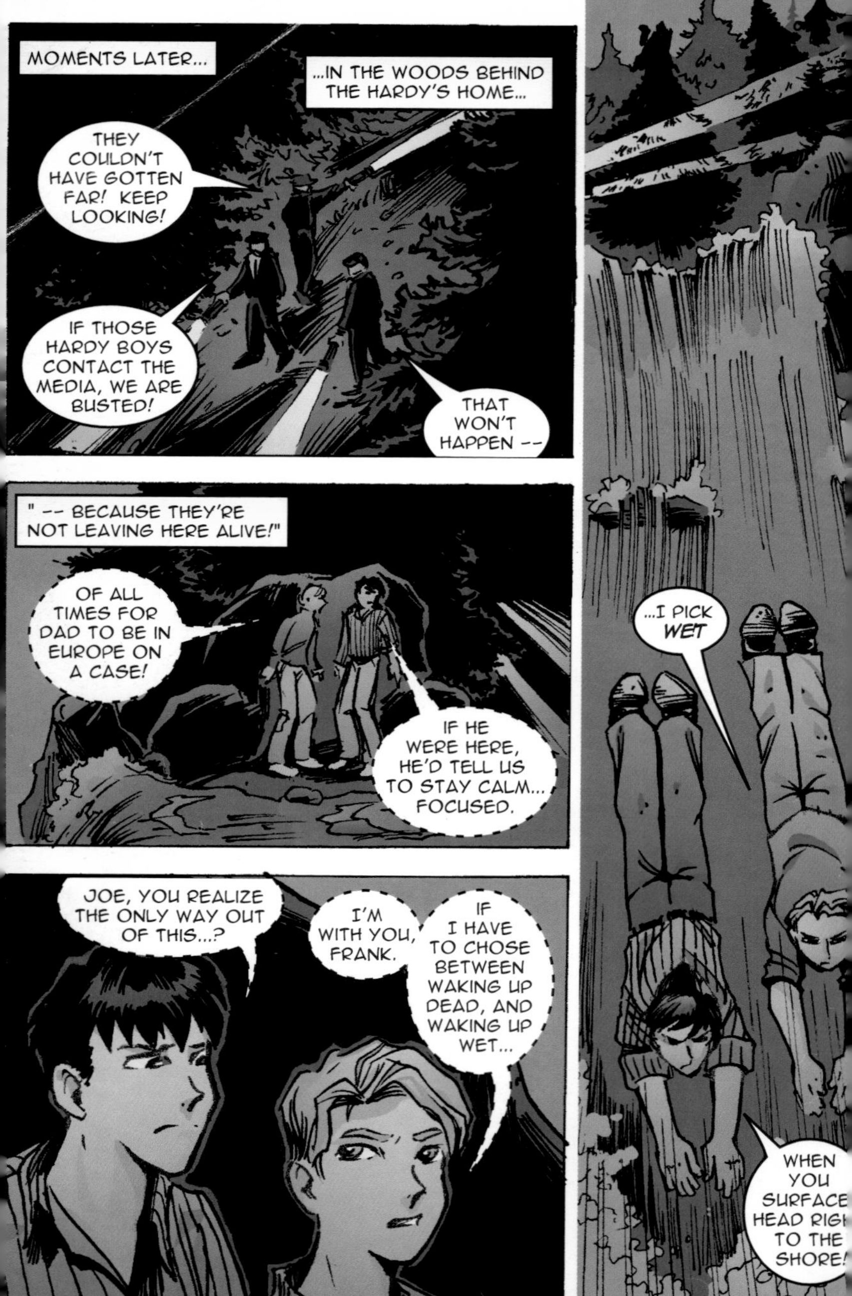
MOMENTS LATER...
...IN THE WOODS BEHIND THE HARDY'S HOME...
THEY COULDN'T HAVE GOTTEN FAR! KEEP LOOKING!
IF THOSE HARDY BOYS CONTACT THE MEDIA, WE ARE BUSTED!
THAT WON'T HAPPEN --
" -- BECAUSE THEY'RE NOT LEAVING HERE ALIVE!"
OF ALL TIMES FOR DAD TO BE IN EUROPE ON A CASE!
IF HE WERE HERE, HE'D TELL US TO STAY CALM... FOCUSED.
JOE, YOU REALIZE THE ONLY WAY OUT OF THIS...?
I'M WITH YOU, FRANK.
IF I HAVE TO CHOSE BETWEEN WAKING UP DEAD, AND WAKING UP WET...
...I PICK WET
WHEN YOU SURFACE HEAD RIG TO THE SHORE!

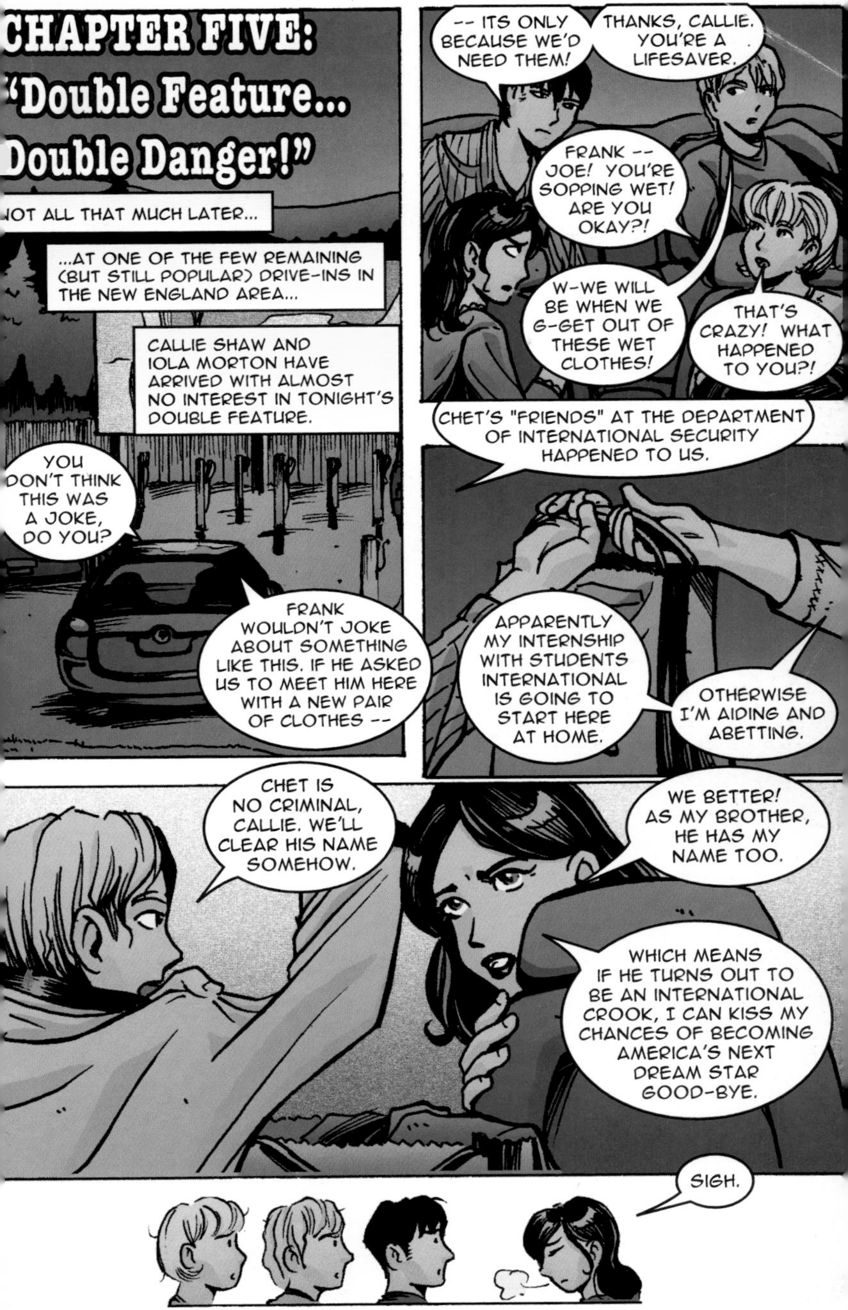
CHAPTER FIVE:
"Double Feature... Double Danger!"
NOT ALL THAT MUCH LATER...
...AT ONE OF THE FEW REMAINING (BUT STILL POPULAR) DRIVE-INS IN THE NEW ENGLAND AREA...
CALLIE SHAW AND IOLA MORTON HAVE ARRIVED WITH ALMOST NO INTEREST IN TONIGHT'S DOUBLE FEATURE.
YOU DON'T THINK THIS WAS A JOKE, DO YOU?
FRANK WOULDN'T JOKE ABOUT SOMETHING LIKE THIS. IF HE ASKED US TO MEET HIM HERE WITH A NEW PAIR OF CLOTHES --
-- ITS ONLY BECAUSE WE'D NEED THEM!
THANKS, CALLIE. YOU'RE A LIFESAVER.
FRANK -- JOE! YOU'RE SOPPING WET! ARE YOU OKAY?!
W-WE WILL BE WHEN WE G-GET OUT OF THESE WET CLOTHES!
THAT'S CRAZY! WHAT HAPPENED TO YOU?!
CHET'S "FRIENDS" AT THE DEPARTMENT OF INTERNATIONAL SECURITY HAPPENED TO US.
APPARENTLY MY INTERNSHIP WITH STUDENTS INTERNATIONAL IS GOING TO START HERE AT HOME.
OTHERWISE I'M AIDING AND ABETTING.
CHET IS NO CRIMINAL, CALLIE. WE'LL CLEAR HIS NAME SOMEHOW.
WE BETTER! AS MY BROTHER, HE HAS MY NAME TOO.
WHICH MEANS IF HE TURNS OUT TO BE AN INTERNATIONAL CROOK, I CAN KISS MY CHANCES OF BECOMING AMERICA'S NEXT DREAM STAR GOOD-BYE.
SIGH.

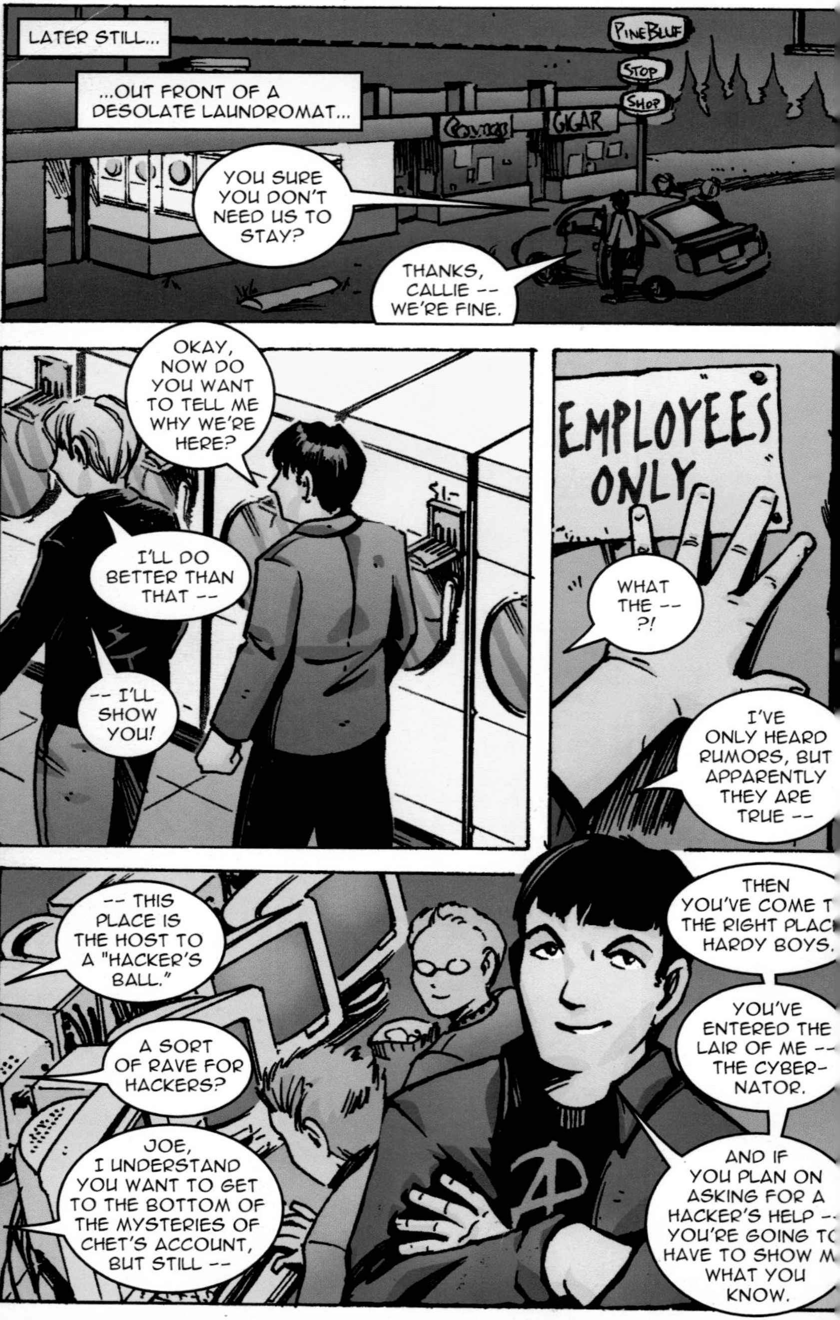
LATER STILL...
...OUT FRONT OF A DESOLATE LAUNDROMAT...
PINE BLUF
STOP
SHOP
GIGAR
YOU SURE YOU DON'T NEED US TO STAY?
THANKS, CALLIE -- WE'RE FINE.
OKAY, NOW DO YOU WANT TO TELL ME WHY WE'RE HERE?
I'LL DO BETTER THAN THAT --
-- I'LL SHOW YOU!
$1.-
EMPLOYEES ONLY
WHAT THE -- ?!
I'VE ONLY HEARD RUMORS, BUT APPARENTLY THEY ARE TRUE --
-- THIS PLACE IS THE HOST TO A "HACKER'S BALL."
A SORT OF RAVE FOR HACKERS?
JOE, I UNDERSTAND YOU WANT TO GET TO THE BOTTOM OF THE MYSTERIES OF CHET'S ACCOUNT, BUT STILL --
THEN YOU'VE COME T THE RIGHT PLAC HARDY BOYS.
YOU'VE ENTERED THE LAIR OF ME -- THE CYBER-NATOR.
AND IF YOU PLAN ON ASKING FOR A HACKER'S HELP -- YOU'RE GOING T HAVE TO SHOW M WHAT YOU KNOW.

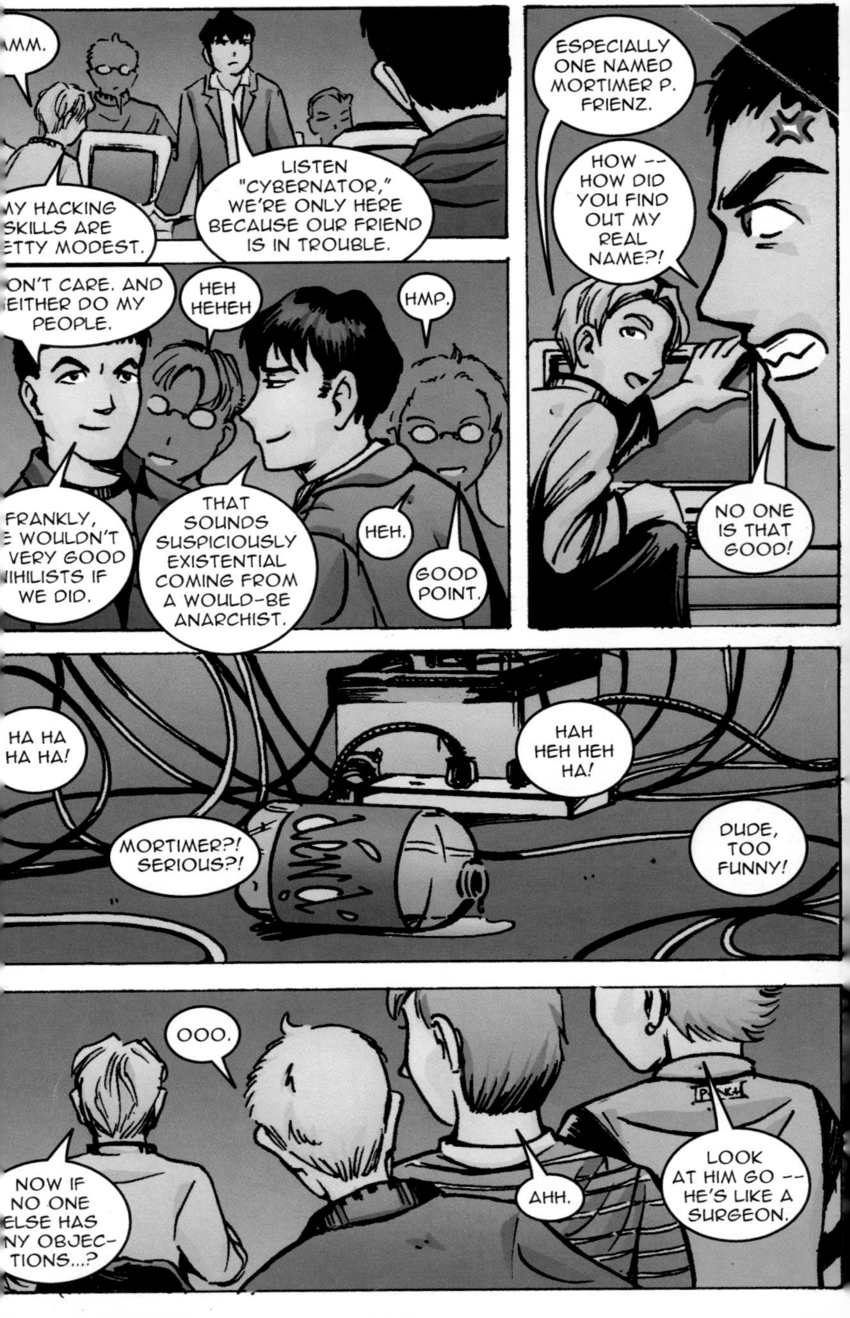

MMM.
MY HACKING SKILLS ARE ETTY MODEST.
LISTEN "CYBERNATOR," WE'RE ONLY HERE BECAUSE OUR FRIEND IS IN TROUBLE.
ESPECIALLY ONE NAMED MORTIMER P. FRIENZ.
HOW -- HOW DID YOU FIND OUT MY REAL NAME?!
NO ONE IS THAT GOOD!
ON'T CARE. AND EITHER DO MY PEOPLE.
HEH HEHEH
HMP.
FRANKLY, E WOULDN'T VERY GOOD IHILISTS IF WE DID.
THAT SOUNDS SUSPICIOUSLY EXISTENTIAL COMING FROM A WOULD-BE ANARCHIST.
HEH.
GOOD POINT.
HA HA HA HA!
HAH HEH HEH HA!
MORTIMER?! SERIOUS?!
DUDE, TOO FUNNY!
OOO.
NOW IF NO ONE ELSE HAS NY OBJEC-TIONS...?
AHH.
LOOK AT HIM GO -- HE'S LIKE A SURGEON.

Location: Osyria

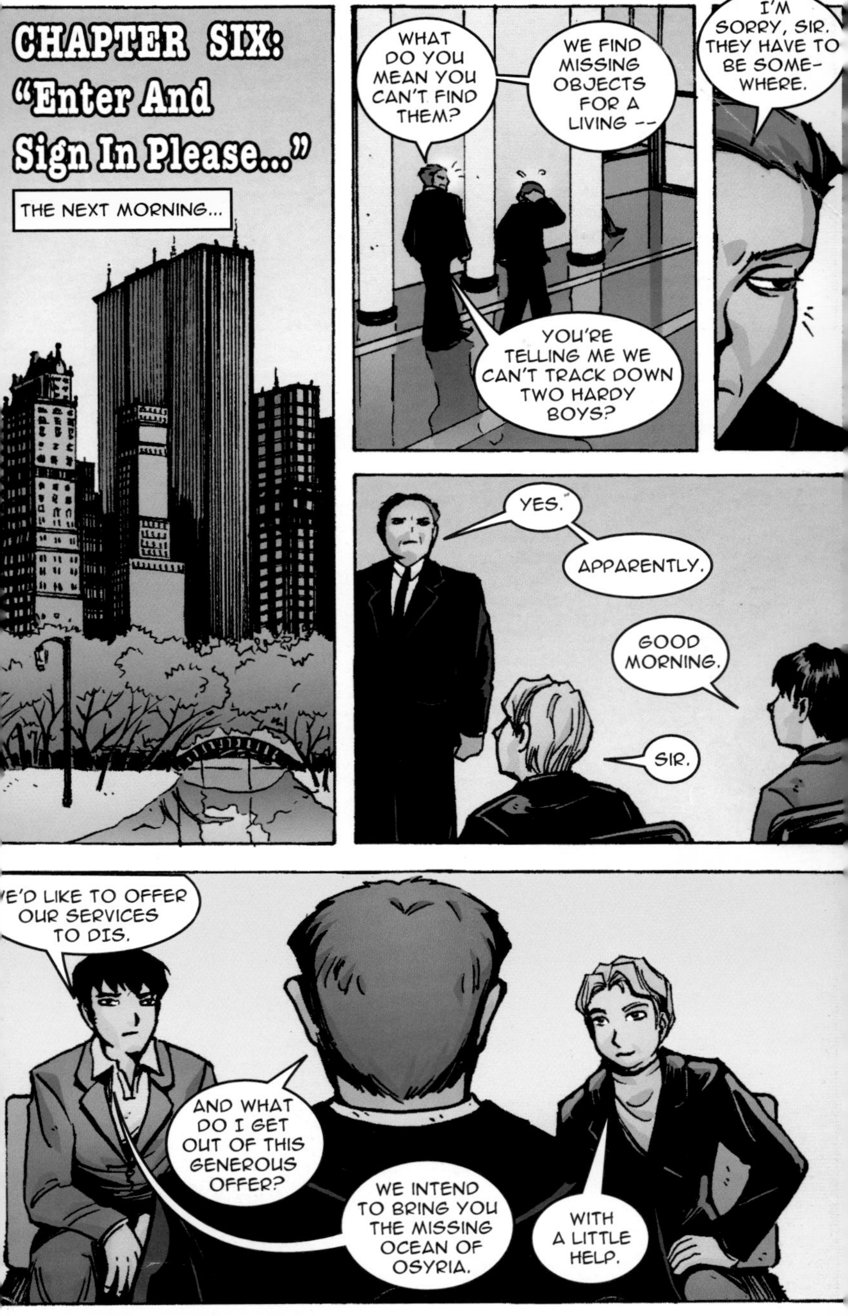

CHAPTER SIX: "Enter And Sign In Please..."
THE NEXT MORNING...
WHAT DO YOU MEAN YOU CAN'T FIND THEM?
WE FIND MISSING OBJECTS FOR A LIVING --
YOU'RE TELLING ME WE CAN'T TRACK DOWN TWO HARDY BOYS?
I'M SORRY, SIR. THEY HAVE TO BE SOME-WHERE.
YES.
APPARENTLY.
GOOD MORNING.
SIR.
E'D LIKE TO OFFER OUR SERVICES TO DIS.
AND WHAT DO I GET OUT OF THIS GENEROUS OFFER?
WE INTEND TO BRING YOU THE MISSING OCEAN OF OSYRIA.
WITH A LITTLE HELP.

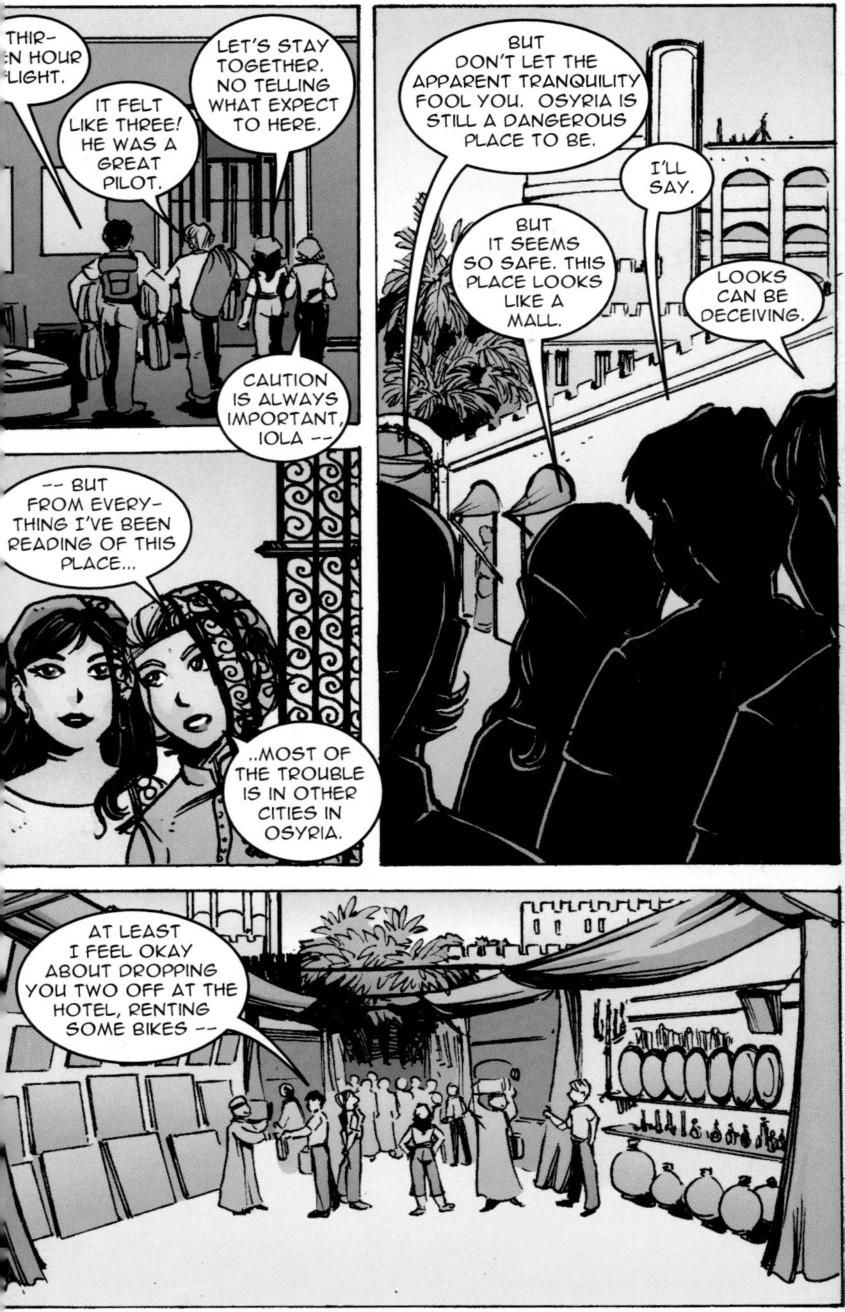
THIR-
EN HOUR
FLIGHT.
IT FELT LIKE THREE! HE WAS A GREAT PILOT.
LET'S STAY TOGETHER. NO TELLING WHAT EXPECT TO HERE.
CAUTION IS ALWAYS IMPORTANT, IOLA --
-- BUT FROM EVERY-THING I'VE BEEN READING OF THIS PLACE...
..MOST OF THE TROUBLE IS IN OTHER CITIES IN OSYRIA.
BUT DON'T LET THE APPARENT TRANQUILITY FOOL YOU. OSYRIA IS STILL A DANGEROUS PLACE TO BE.
I'LL SAY.
BUT IT SEEMS SO SAFE. THIS PLACE LOOKS LIKE A MALL.
LOOKS CAN BE DECEIVING.
AT LEAST I FEEL OKAY ABOUT DROPPING YOU TWO OFF AT THE HOTEL, RENTING SOME BIKES --

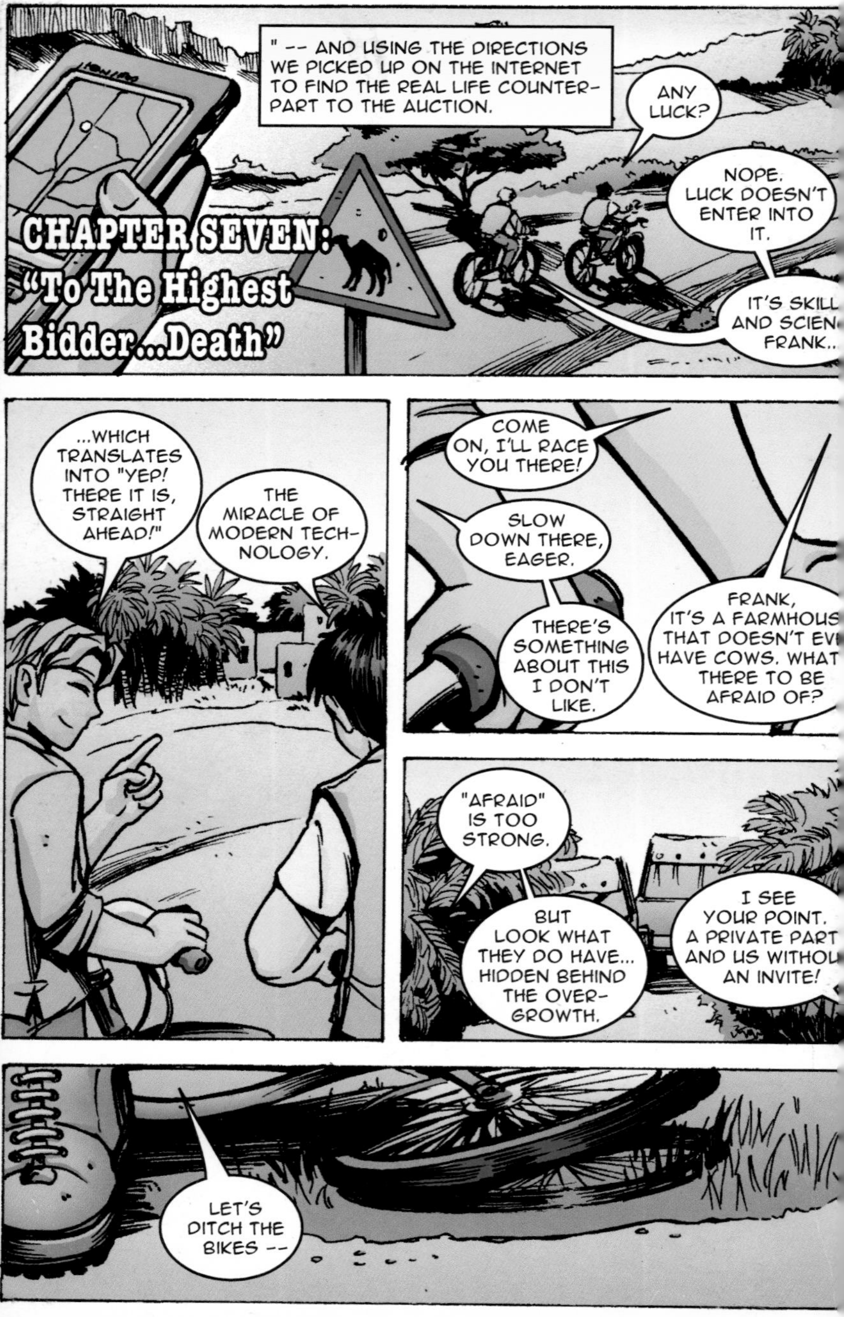
" -- AND USING THE DIRECTIONS WE PICKED UP ON THE INTERNET TO FIND THE REAL LIFE COUNTER-PART TO THE AUCTION.
ANY LUCK?
NOPE. LUCK DOESN'T ENTER INTO IT.
IT'S SKILL AND SCIEN FRANK...
CHAPTER SEVEN: "To The Highest Bidder...Death"
...WHICH TRANSLATES INTO "YEP! THERE IT IS, STRAIGHT AHEAD!"
THE MIRACLE OF MODERN TECH-NOLOGY.
COME ON, I'LL RACE YOU THERE!
SLOW DOWN THERE, EAGER.
THERE'S SOMETHING ABOUT THIS I DON'T LIKE.
FRANK, IT'S A FARMHOUS THAT DOESN'T EV HAVE COWS. WHAT THERE TO BE AFRAID OF?
"AFRAID" IS TOO STRONG.
BUT LOOK WHAT THEY DO HAVE... HIDDEN BEHIND THE OVER-GROWTH.
I SEE YOUR POINT. A PRIVATE PART AND US WITHOU AN INVITE!
LET'S DITCH THE BIKES --

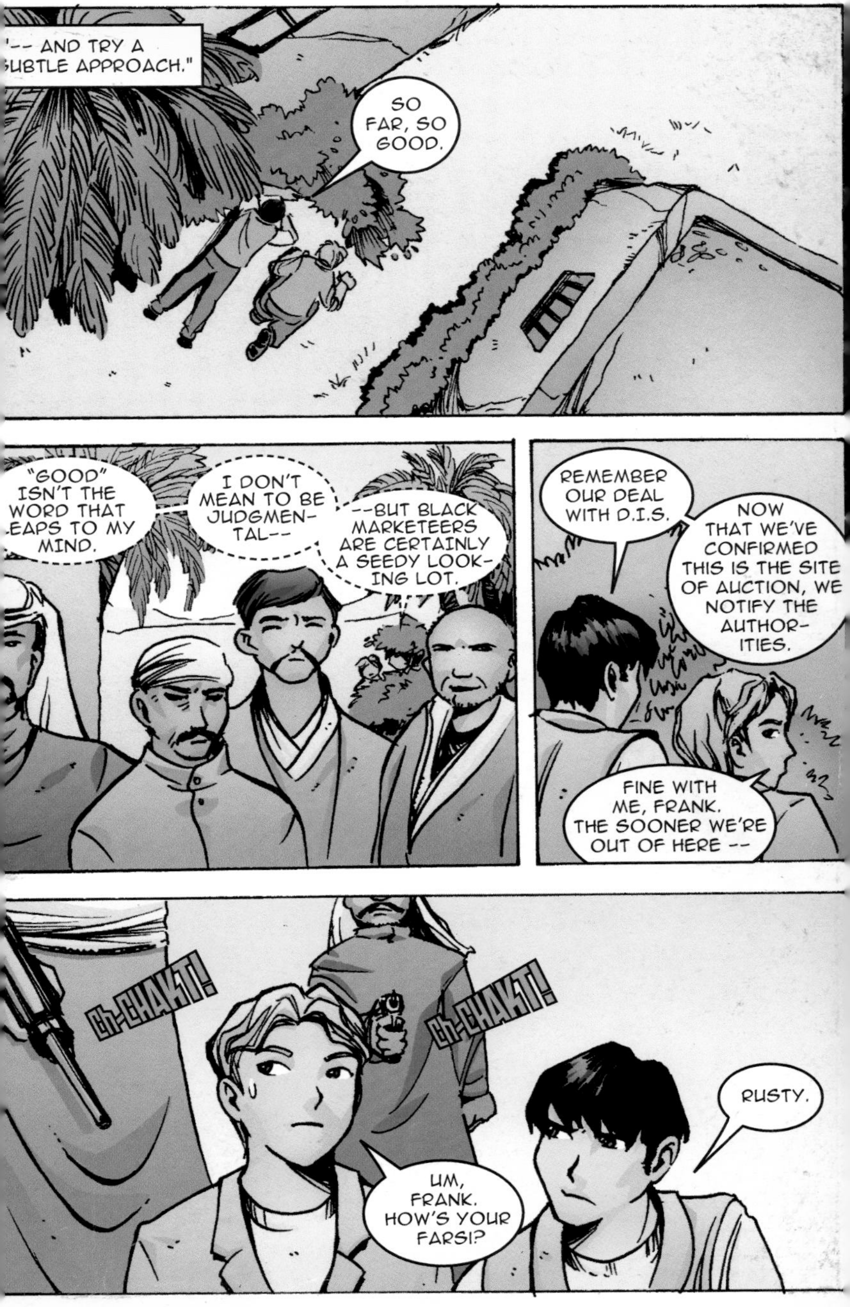
"-- AND TRY A
SUBTLE APPROACH."
SO FAR, SO GOOD.
"GOOD" ISN'T THE WORD THAT LEAPS TO MY MIND.
I DON'T MEAN TO BE JUDGMENTAL--
--BUT BLACK MARKETEERS ARE CERTAINLY A SEEDY LOOKING LOT.
REMEMBER OUR DEAL WITH D.I.S.
NOW THAT WE'VE CONFIRMED THIS IS THE SITE OF AUCTION, WE NOTIFY THE AUTHORITIES.
FINE WITH ME, FRANK. THE SOONER WE'RE OUT OF HERE --
CH-CHAKT!
CH-CHAKT!
UM, FRANK. HOW'S YOUR FARSI?
RUSTY.

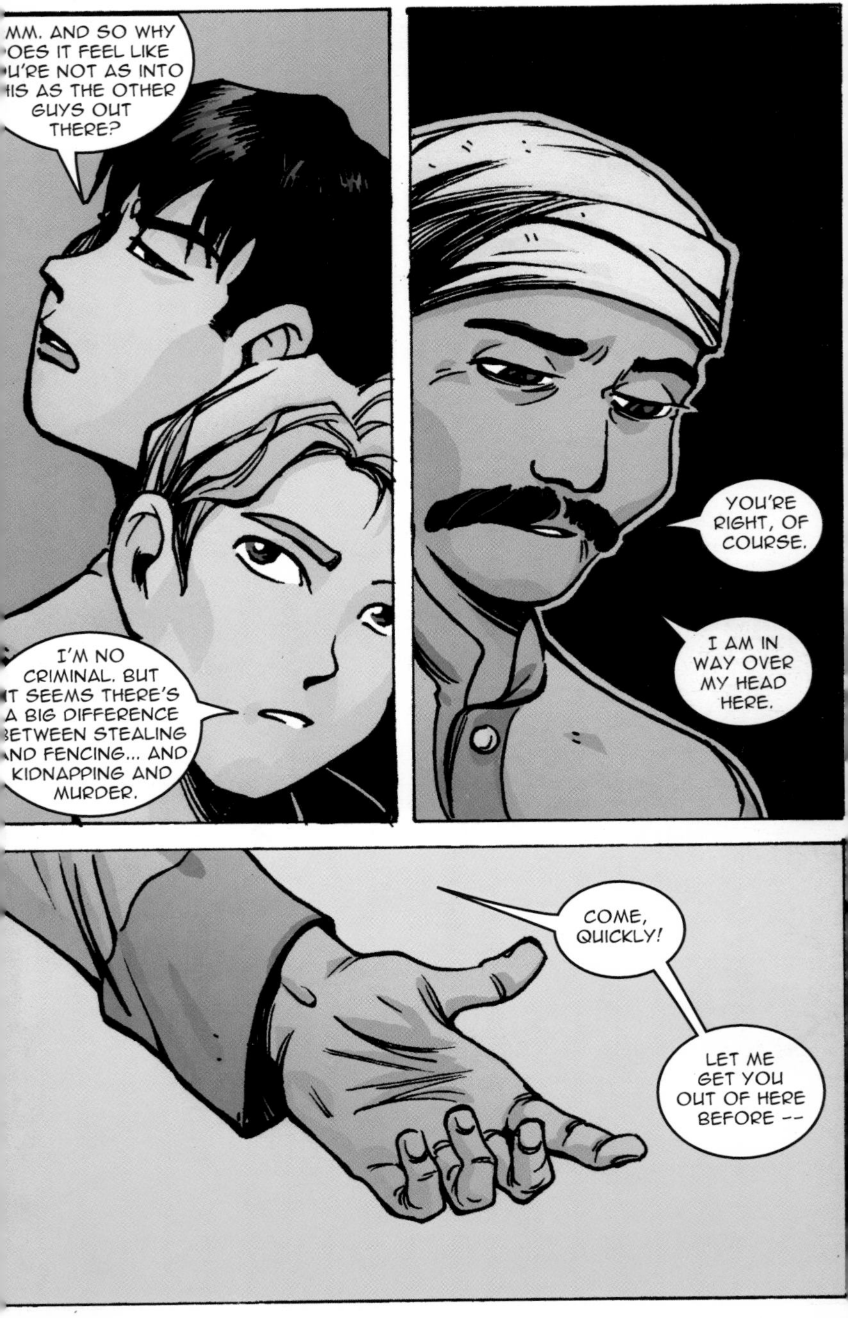
MM. AND SO WHY OES IT FEEL LIKE U'RE NOT AS INTO IS AS THE OTHER GUYS OUT THERE?
I'M NO CRIMINAL. BUT IT SEEMS THERE'S A BIG DIFFERENCE ETWEEN STEALING ND FENCING... AND KIDNAPPING AND MURDER.
YOU'RE RIGHT, OF COURSE.
I AM IN WAY OVER MY HEAD HERE.
COME, QUICKLY!
LET ME GET YOU OUT OF HERE BEFORE --

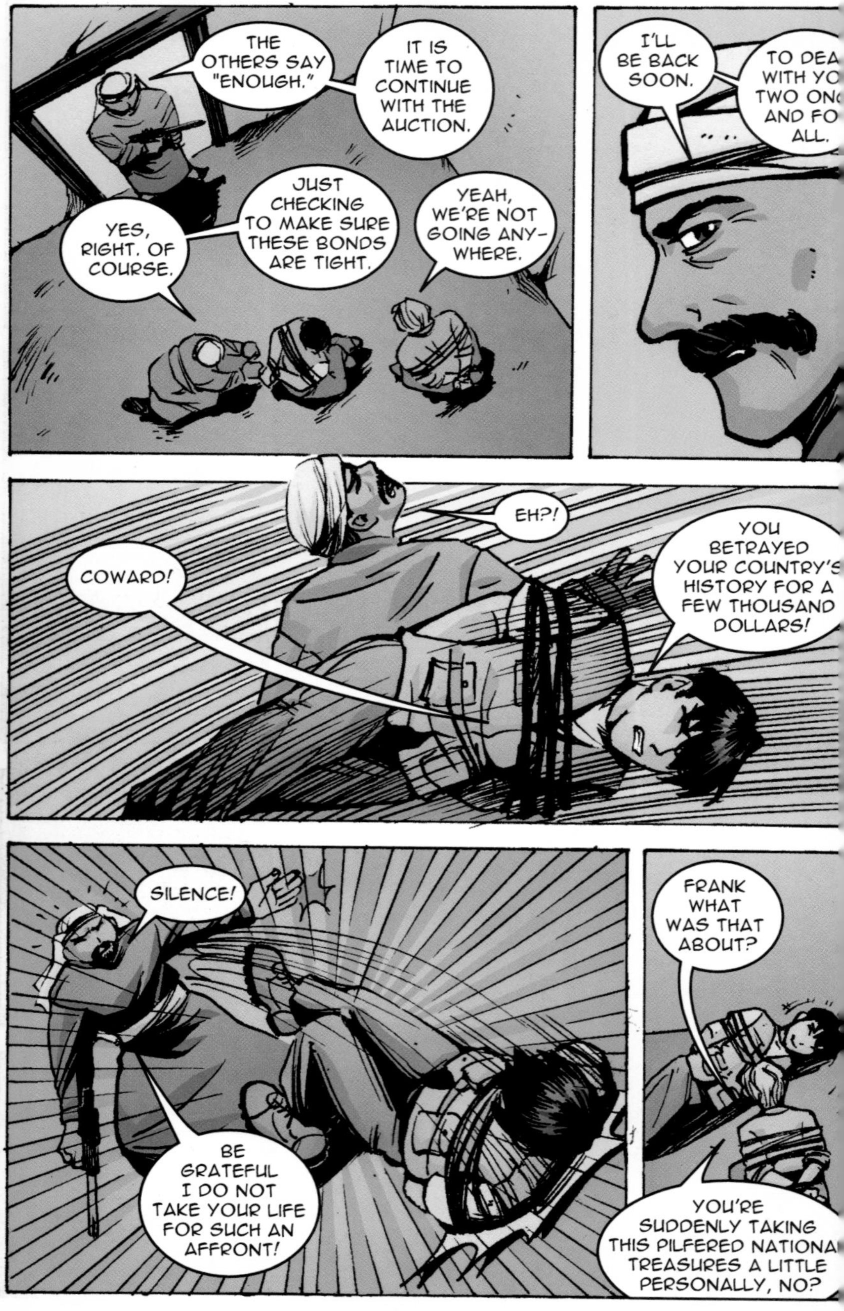
THE OTHERS SAY "ENOUGH."
IT IS TIME TO CONTINUE WITH THE AUCTION.
YES, RIGHT. OF COURSE.
JUST CHECKING TO MAKE SURE THESE BONDS ARE TIGHT.
YEAH, WE'RE NOT GOING ANY-WHERE.
I'LL BE BACK SOON.
...
EH?!
COWARD!
YOU BETRAYED YOUR COUNTRY'S HISTORY FOR A FEW THOUSAND DOLLARS!
SILENCE!
BE GRATEFUL I DO NOT TAKE YOUR LIFE FOR SUCH AN AFFRONT!
FRANK WHAT WAS THAT ABOUT?
YOU'RE SUDDENLY TAKING THIS PILFERED NATIONA TREASURES A LITTLE PERSONALLY, NO?

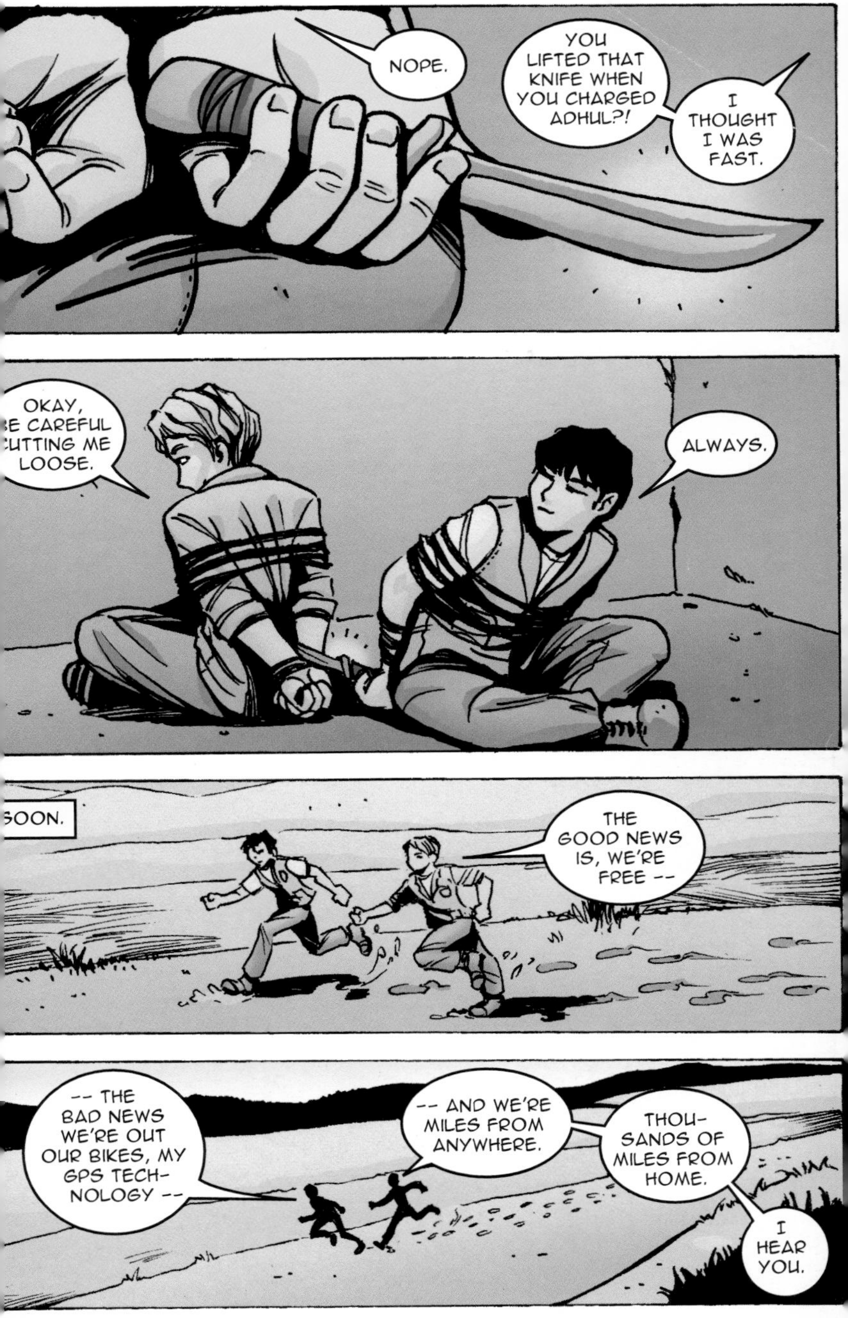
NOPE.
YOU LIFTED THAT KNIFE WHEN YOU CHARGED ADHUL?!
I THOUGHT I WAS FAST.
OKAY, BE CAREFUL CUTTING ME LOOSE.
ALWAYS.
SOON.
THE GOOD NEWS IS, WE'RE FREE --
-- THE BAD NEWS WE'RE OUT OUR BIKES, MY GPS TECH-NOLOGY --
-- AND WE'RE MILES FROM ANYWHERE.
THOU-SANDS OF MILES FROM HOME.
I HEAR YOU.

CHAPTER EIGHT:
"An Ocean In The Hand..."

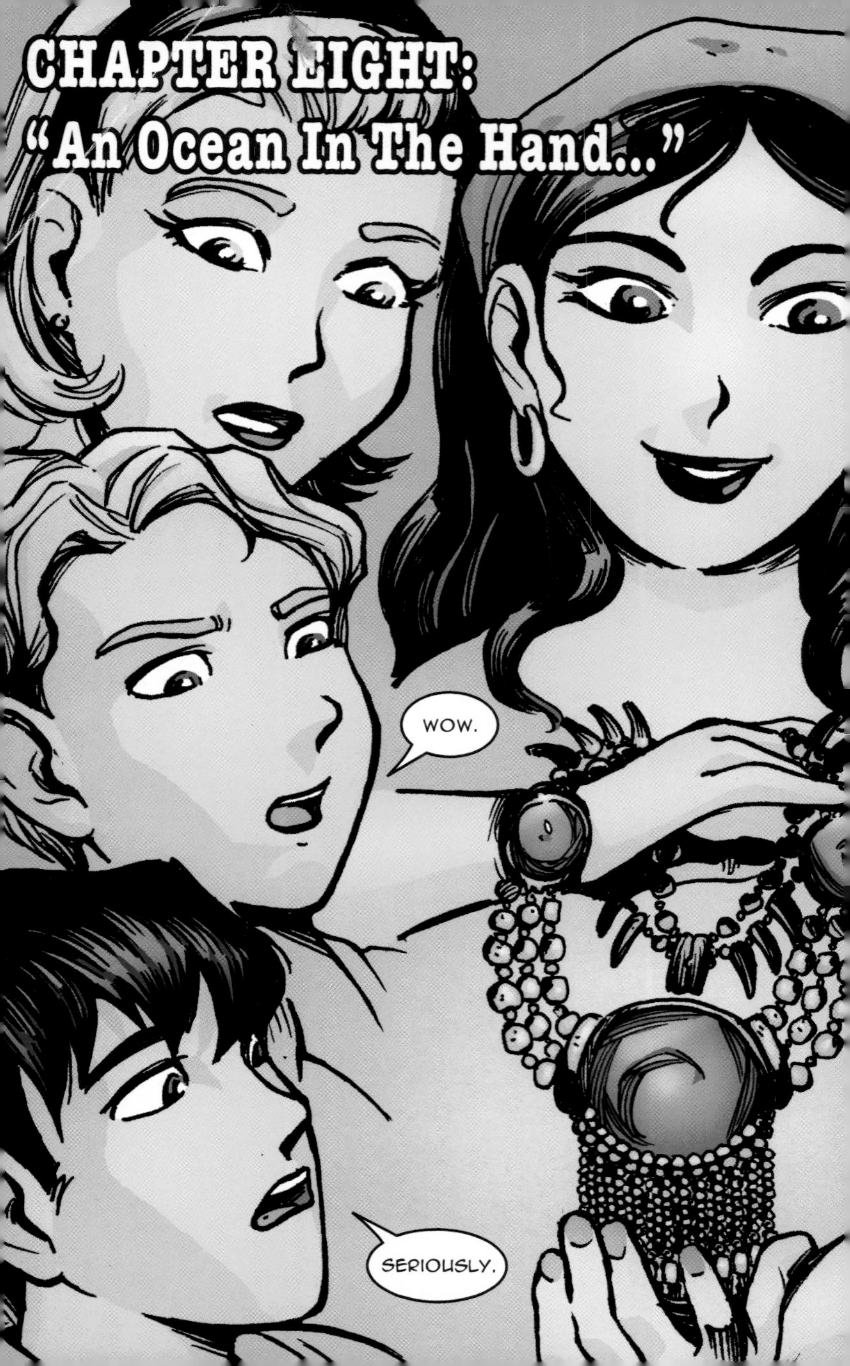
WOW.
SERIOUSLY.

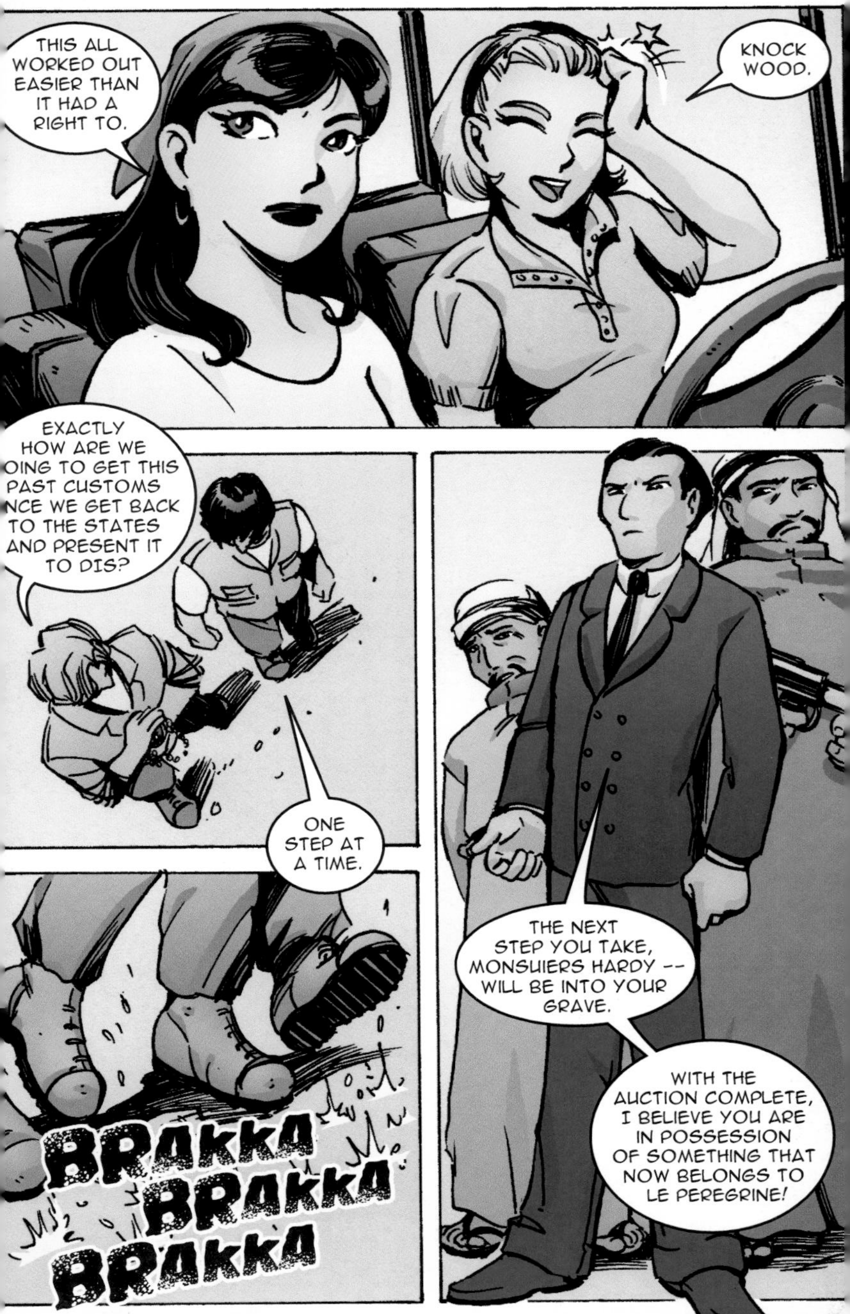
THIS ALL WORKED OUT EASIER THAN IT HAD A RIGHT TO.
KNOCK WOOD.
EXACTLY HOW ARE WE OING TO GET THIS PAST CUSTOMS NCE WE GET BACK TO THE STATES AND PRESENT IT TO DIS?
ONE STEP AT A TIME.
BRAKKA BRAKKA BRAKKA
THE NEXT STEP YOU TAKE, MONSUIERS HARDY -- WILL BE INTO YOUR GRAVE.
WITH THE AUCTION COMPLETE, I BELIEVE YOU ARE IN POSSESSION OF SOMETHING THAT NOW BELONGS TO LE PEREGRINE!

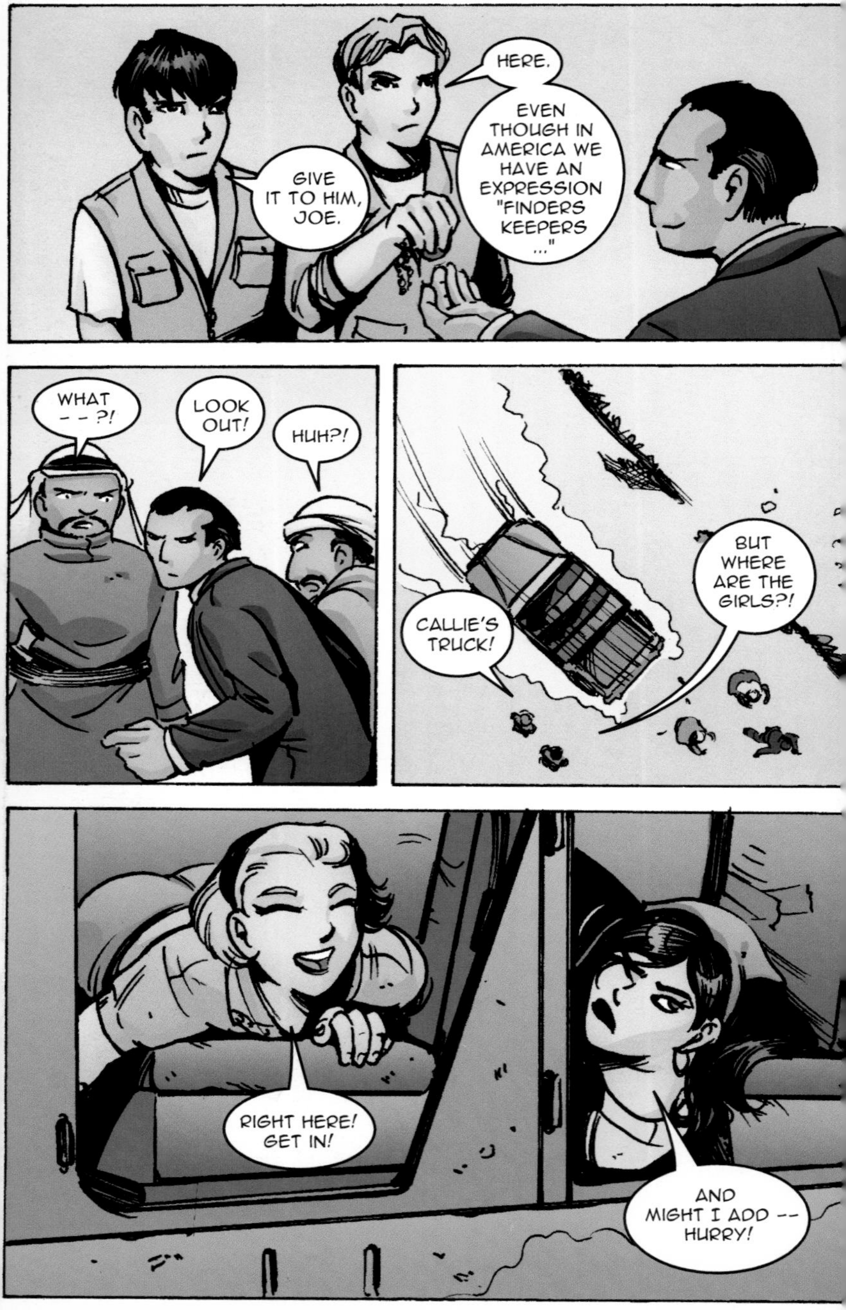
HERE.
EVEN THOUGH IN AMERICA WE HAVE AN EXPRESSION "FINDERS KEEPERS ..."
GIVE IT TO HIM, JOE.
WHAT --?!
LOOK OUT!
HUH?!
CALLIE'S TRUCK!
BUT WHERE ARE THE GIRLS?!
RIGHT HERE! GET IN!
AND MIGHT I ADD -- HURRY!

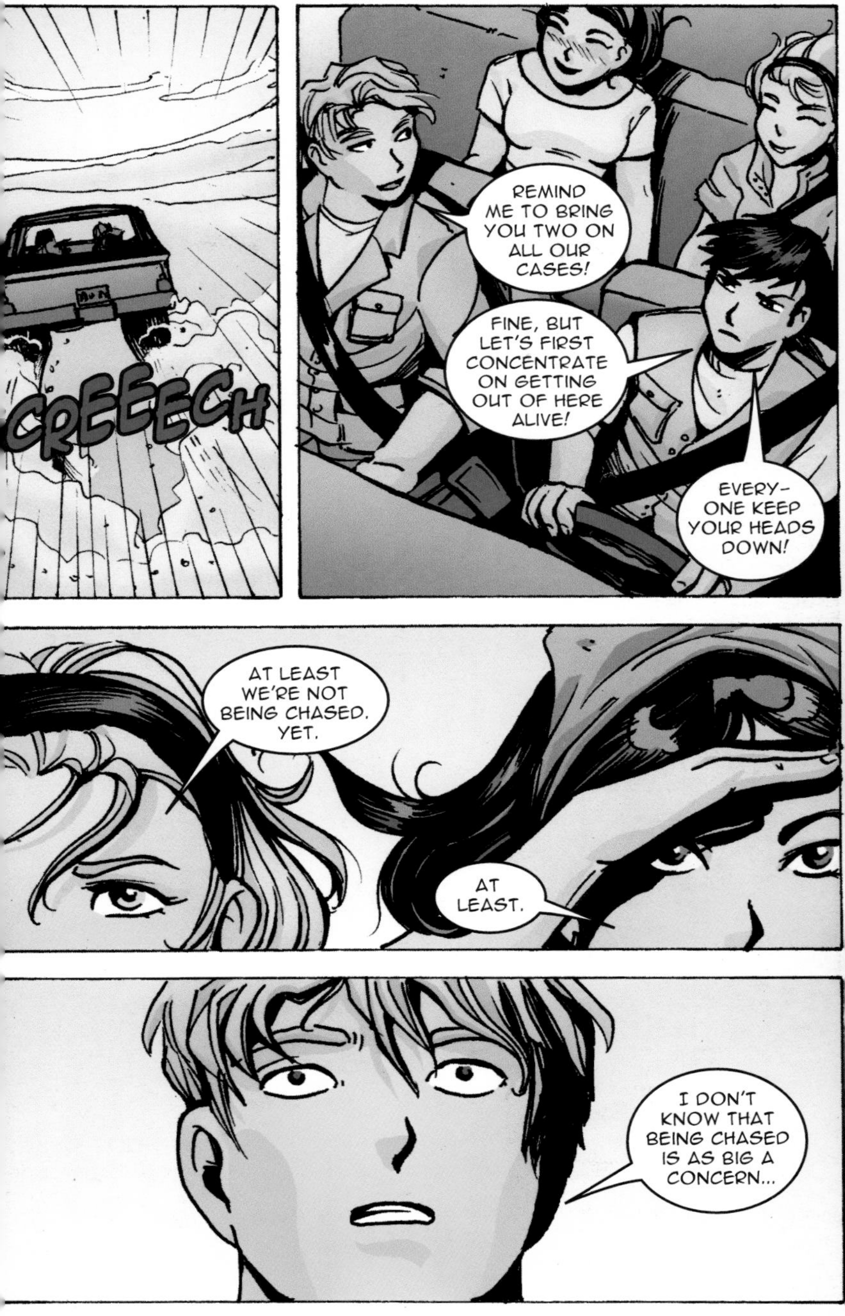
CREEECH
REMIND ME TO BRING YOU TWO ON ALL OUR CASES!
FINE, BUT LET'S FIRST CONCENTRATE ON GETTING OUT OF HERE ALIVE!
EVERY-ONE KEEP YOUR HEADS DOWN!
AT LEAST WE'RE NOT BEING CHASED. YET.
AT LEAST.
I DON'T KNOW THAT BEING CHASED IS AS BIG A CONCERN...

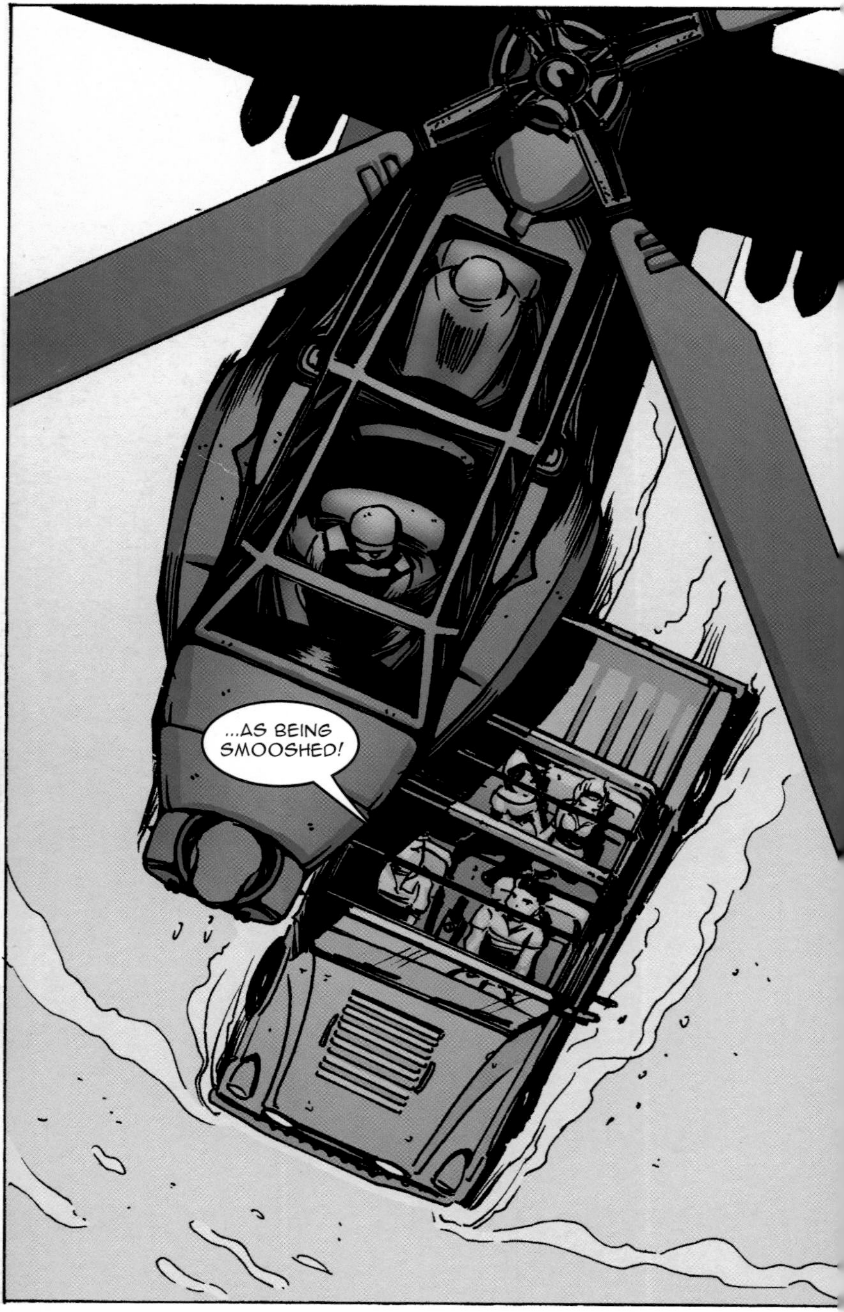
...AS BEING SMOOSHED!

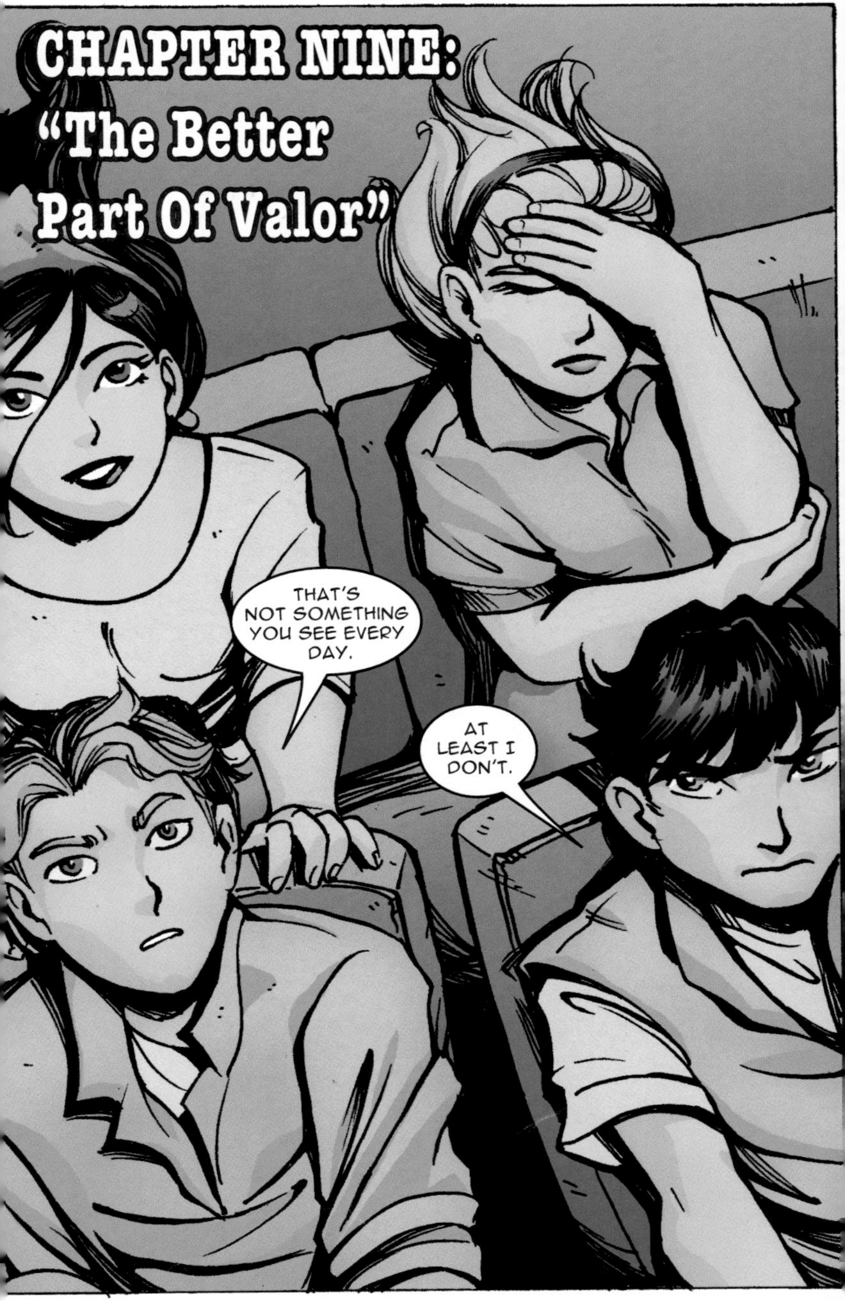
CHAPTER NINE:
"The Better Part Of Valor"
THAT'S NOT SOMETHING YOU SEE EVERY DAY.
AT LEAST I DON'T.

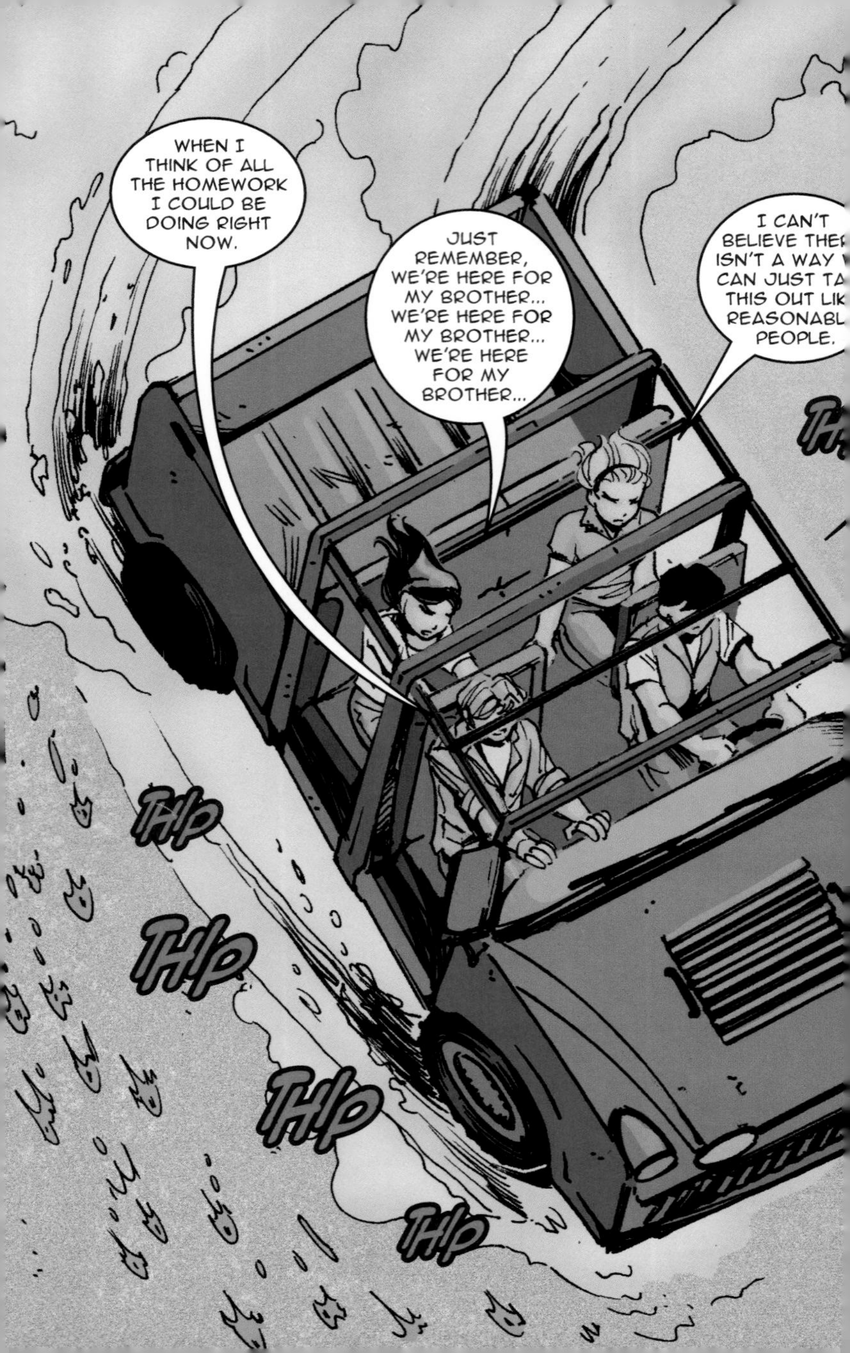
WHEN I THINK OF ALL THE HOMEWORK I COULD BE DOING RIGHT NOW.
JUST REMEMBER, WE'RE HERE FOR MY BROTHER... WE'RE HERE FOR MY BROTHER... WE'RE HERE FOR MY BROTHER...
THP
THP
THP
THP

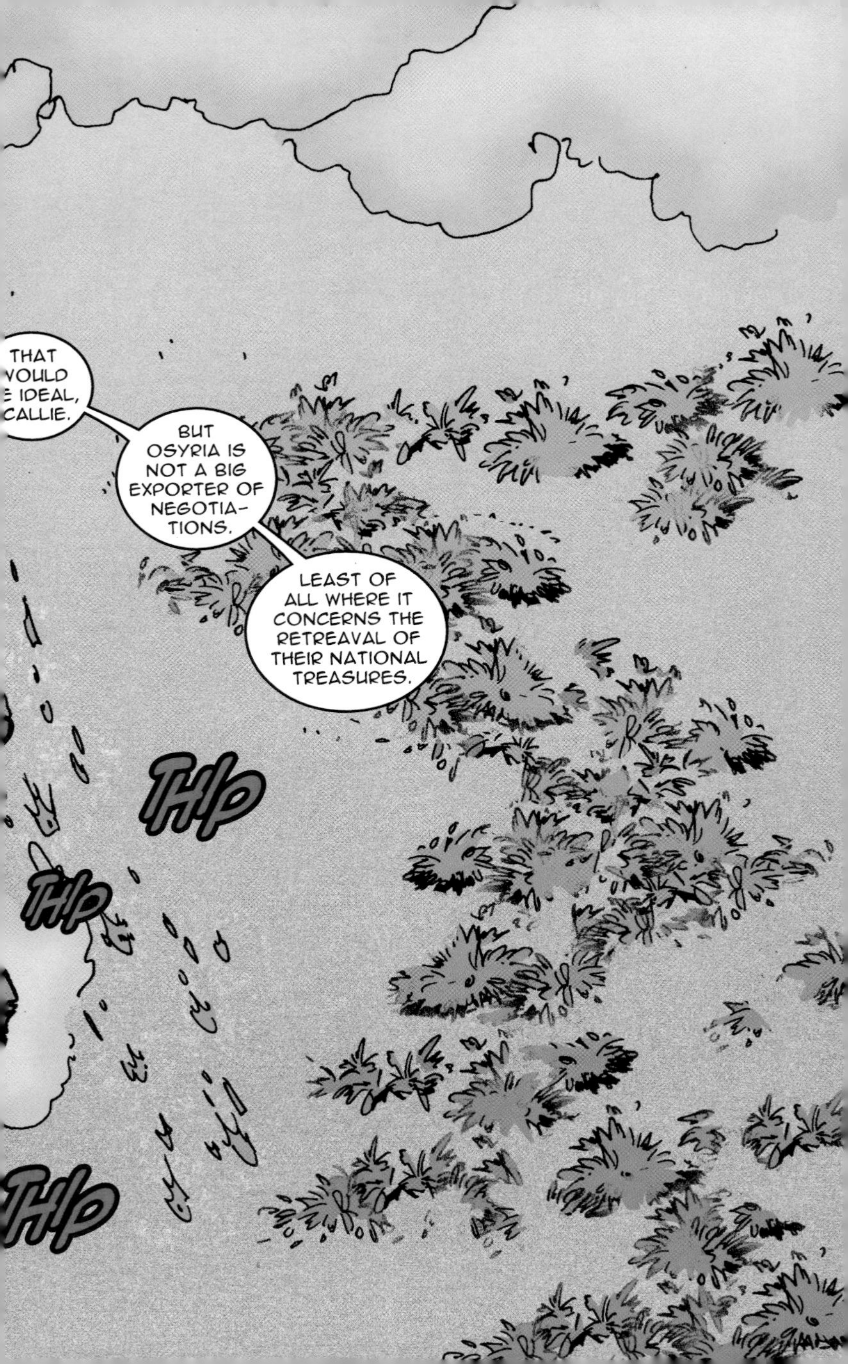
THAT WOULD BE IDEAL, CALLIE.
BUT OSYRIA IS NOT A BIG EXPORTER OF NEGOTIA- TIONS.
LEAST OF ALL WHERE IT CONCERNS THE RETREAVAL OF THEIR NATIONAL TREASURES.
THP
THP
THP

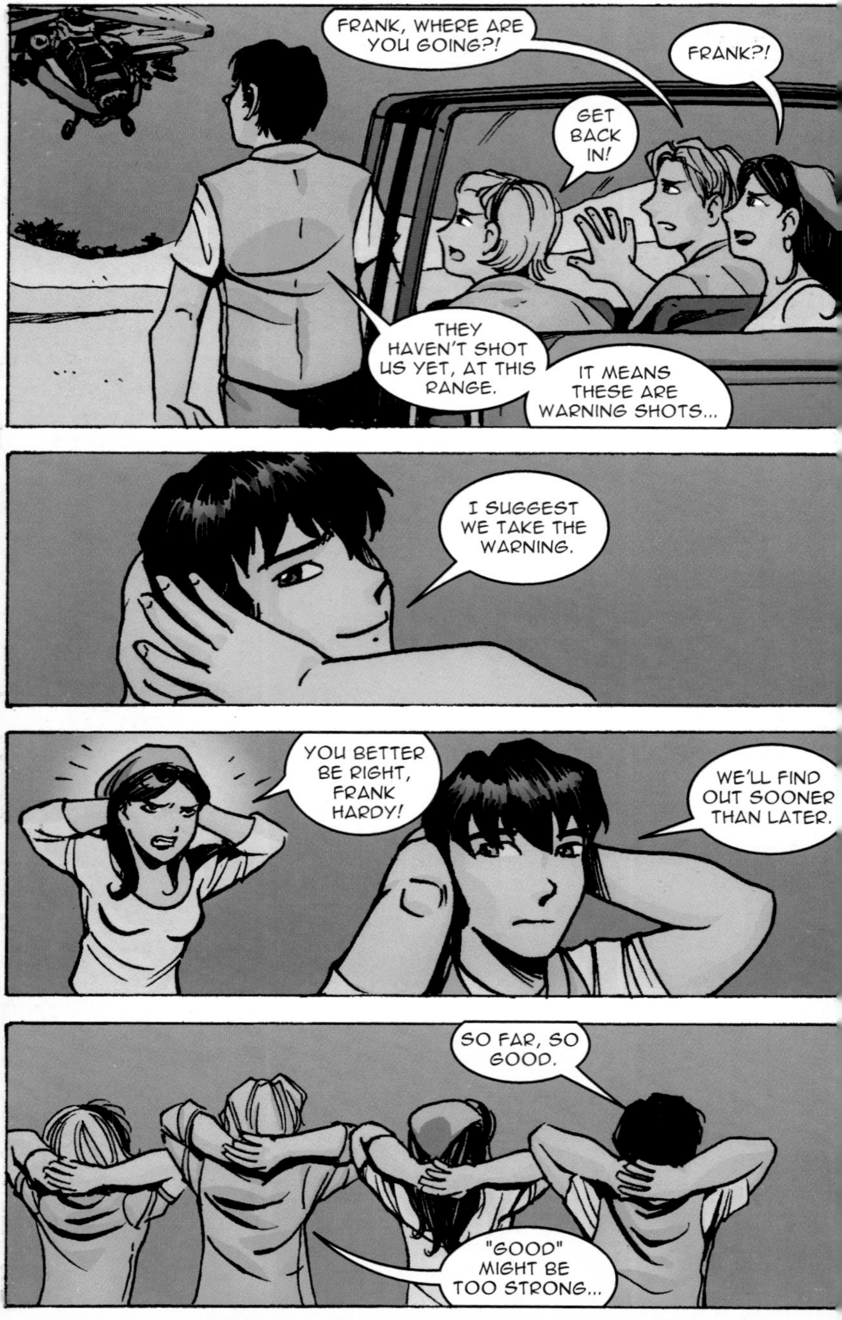
FRANK, WHERE ARE YOU GOING?!
FRANK?!
GET BACK IN!
THEY HAVEN'T SHOT US YET, AT THIS RANGE.
IT MEANS THESE ARE WARNING SHOTS...
I SUGGEST WE TAKE THE WARNING.
YOU BETTER BE RIGHT, FRANK HARDY!
WE'LL FIND OUT SOONER THAN LATER.
SO FAR, SO GOOD.
"GOOD" MIGHT BE TOO STRONG...

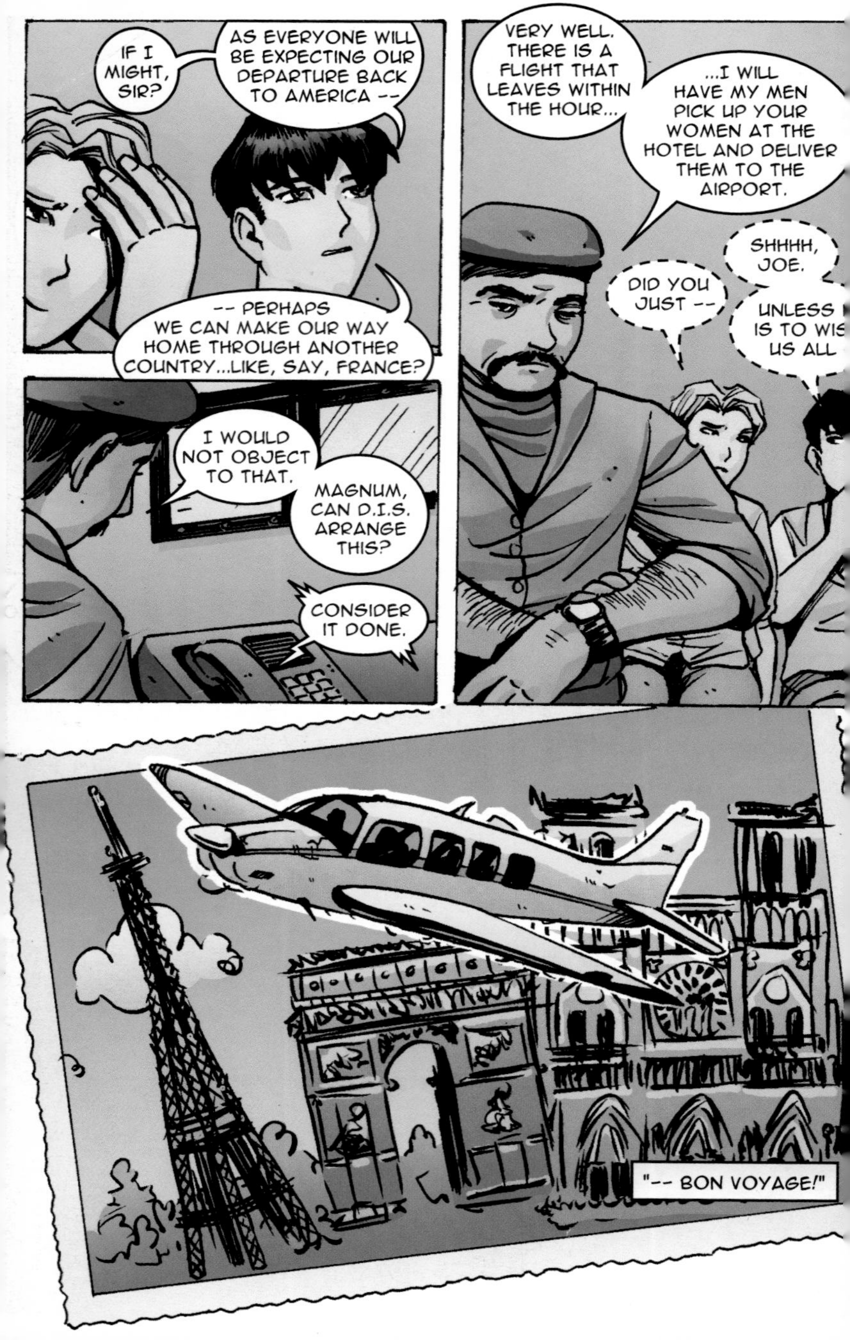
IF I MIGHT, SIR?
AS EVERYONE WILL BE EXPECTING OUR DEPARTURE BACK TO AMERICA --
-- PERHAPS WE CAN MAKE OUR WAY HOME THROUGH ANOTHER COUNTRY...LIKE, SAY, FRANCE?
I WOULD NOT OBJECT TO THAT.
MAGNUM, CAN D.I.S. ARRANGE THIS?
CONSIDER IT DONE.
VERY WELL. THERE IS A FLIGHT THAT LEAVES WITHIN THE HOUR...
...I WILL HAVE MY MEN PICK UP YOUR WOMEN AT THE HOTEL AND DELIVER THEM TO THE AIRPORT.
DID YOU JUST --
SHHHH, JOE.
"-- BON VOYAGE!"

CHAPTER TEN:
"The French Are Different Than You and I"

THINK OF IT AS A WAY OF KEEPING UP ON YOUR SCHOOL WORK WHILE WE'RE ABROAD.

THEN GIVE ME AN "A+," FRANK --

-- BECAUSE I'VE FOUND THE IDENTITY OF THE MAN YOU AND I MET EARLIER UNDER HIS ALIAS, LE PEREGRINE.

HIS NAME IS LAURENT ST. LAURENT...

...AND HE'S ESTIMATED TO BE ONE OF THE RICHEST MEN IN FRANCE.

ARE YOU KIDDING?!

IOLA?

ACCORDING TO HIS PRESS, HE CAME BY HIS MONEY THROUGH INVESTMENTS IN COSMETIC AND BOOK PUBLISHING VENTURES.

DOES THAT SAY HE'S HAVING A FUND RAISER TONIGHT AT HIS MANSION ALONG THE RIVER SEINE?

FINALLY I GET TO BE USEFUL! THE ONE THING I CAN DO ON EITHER SIDE OF THE ATLANTIC --

NOT THAT WE HAVE ANY WAY TO GET THERE.

-- IS TO GET US INTO A PARTY!

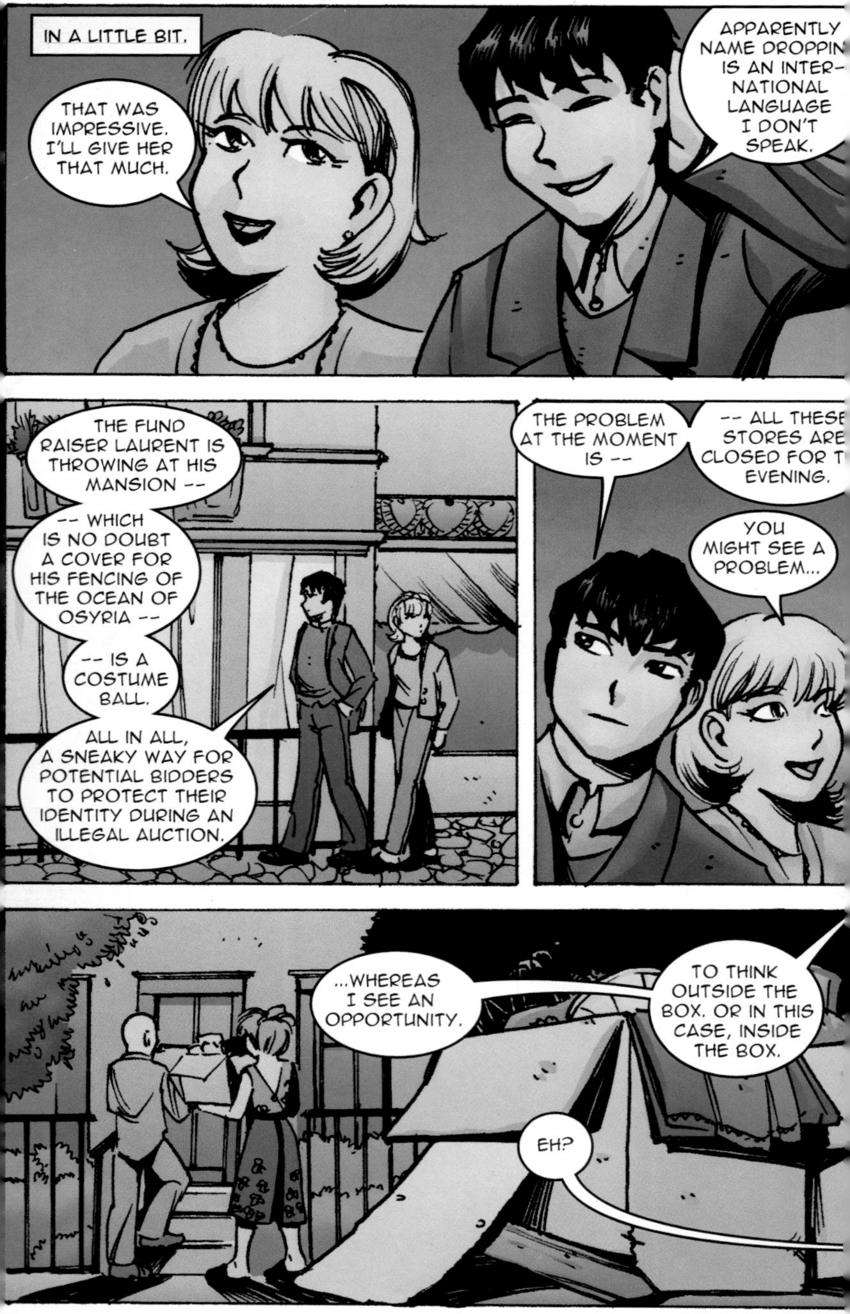
IN A LITTLE BIT.
THAT WAS IMPRESSIVE. I'LL GIVE HER THAT MUCH.
APPARENTLY NAME DROPPIN IS AN INTER-NATIONAL LANGUAGE I DON'T SPEAK.
THE FUND RAISER LAURENT IS THROWING AT HIS MANSION --
-- WHICH IS NO DOUBT A COVER FOR HIS FENCING OF THE OCEAN OF OSYRIA --
-- IS A COSTUME BALL.
ALL IN ALL, A SNEAKY WAY FOR POTENTIAL BIDDERS TO PROTECT THEIR IDENTITY DURING AN ILLEGAL AUCTION.
THE PROBLEM AT THE MOMENT IS --
-- ALL THESE STORES ARE CLOSED FOR T EVENING.
YOU MIGHT SEE A PROBLEM...
...WHEREAS I SEE AN OPPORTUNITY.
TO THINK OUTSIDE THE BOX. OR IN THIS CASE, INSIDE THE BOX.
EH?

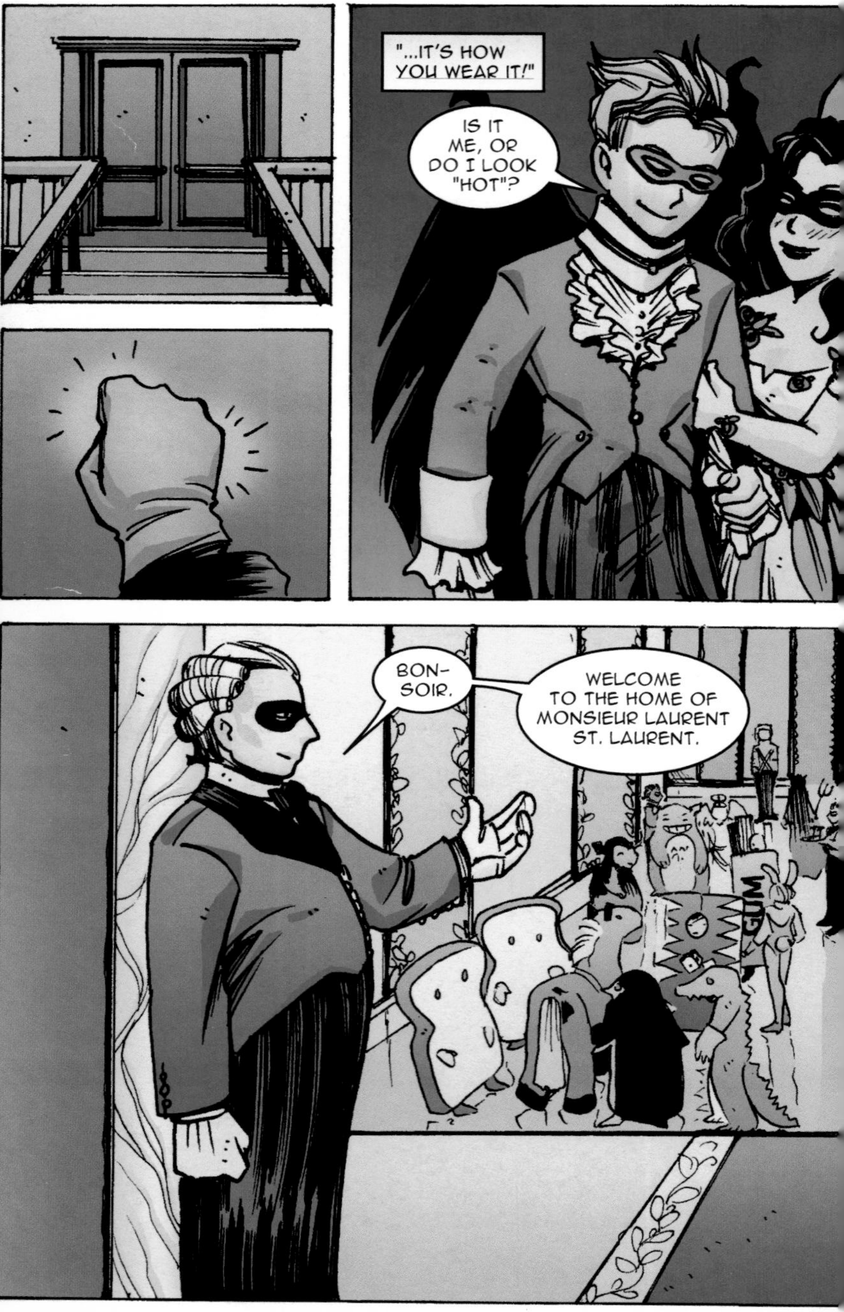
"...IT'S HOW YOU WEAR IT!"
IS IT ME, OR DO I LOOK "HOT"?
BON-SOIR.
WELCOME TO THE HOME OF MONSIEUR LAURENT ST. LAURENT.
GUM

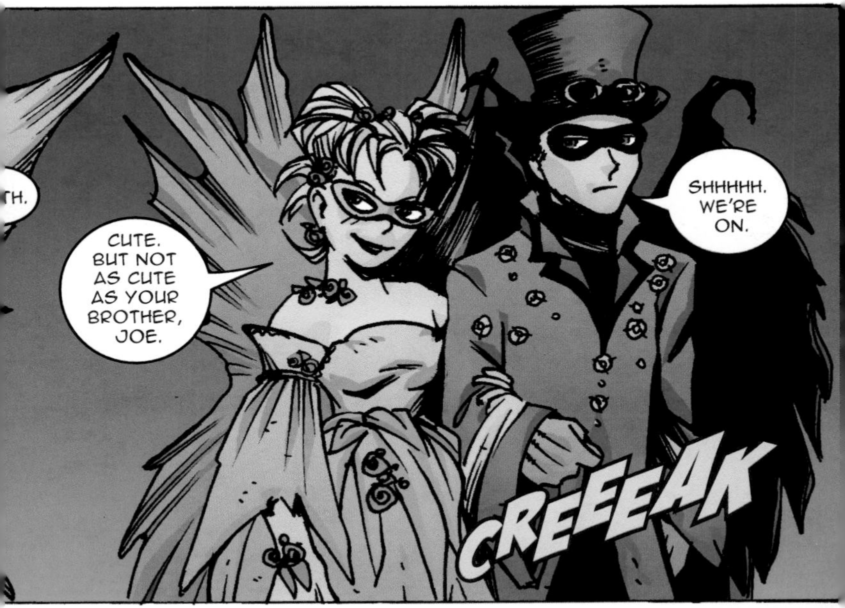
TH.
CUTE. BUT NOT AS CUTE AS YOUR BROTHER, JOE.
SHHHHH. WE'RE ON.
CREEEAK
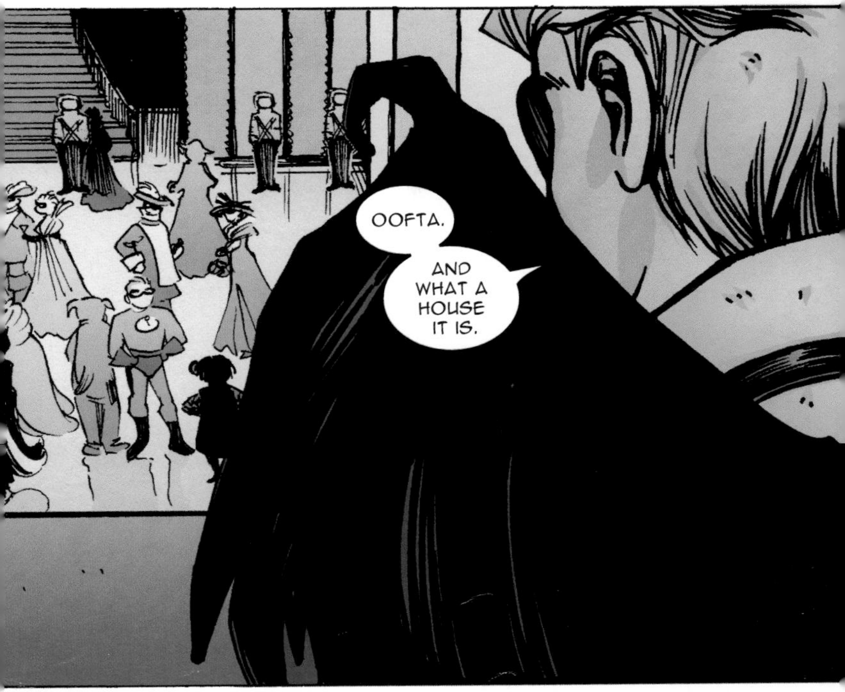
OOFTA.
AND WHAT A HOUSE IT IS.

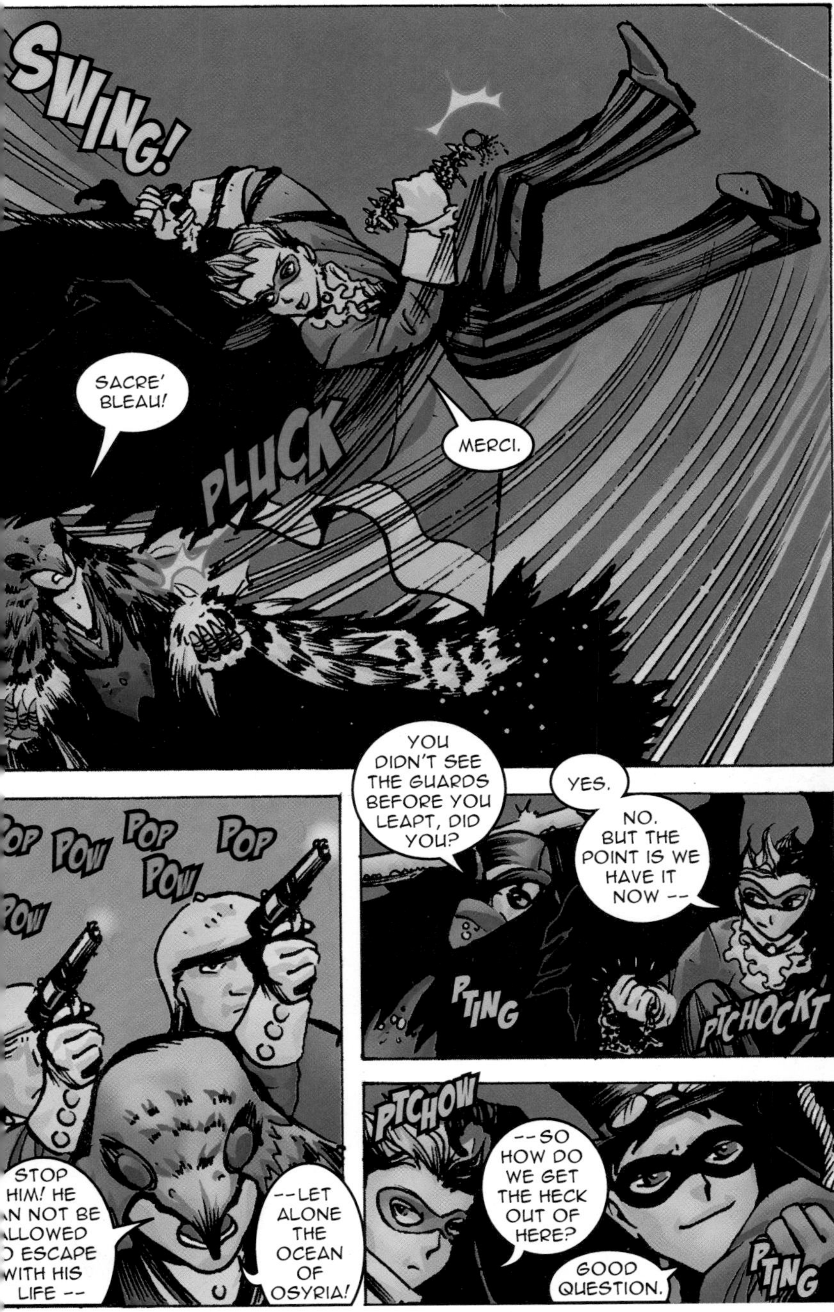
SWING!
SACRE' BLEAU!
PLUCK
MERCI.
YOU DIDN'T SEE THE GUARDS BEFORE YOU LEAPT, DID YOU?
YES.
NO. BUT THE POINT IS WE HAVE IT NOW --
PTING
PTCHOCKT
POP POW POP POP POW POW
STOP HIM! HE AN NOT BE ALLOWED O ESCAPE WITH HIS LIFE --
--LET ALONE THE OCEAN OF OSYRIA!
PTCHOW
--SO HOW DO WE GET THE HECK OUT OF HERE?
GOOD QUESTION.
PTING

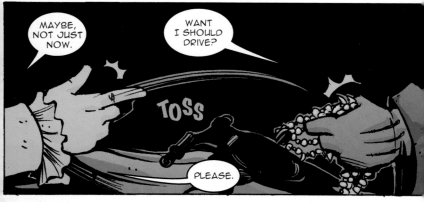

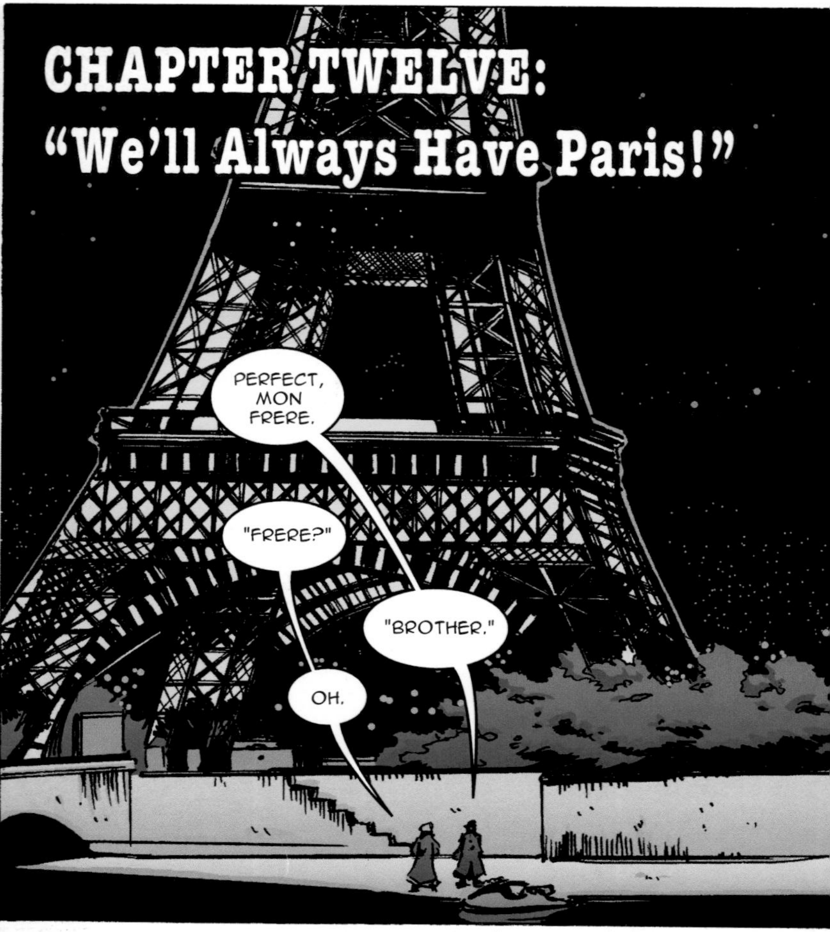
CHAPTER TWELVE:
"We'll Always Have Paris!"
PERFECT, MON FRERE.
"FRERE?"
"BROTHER."
OH.

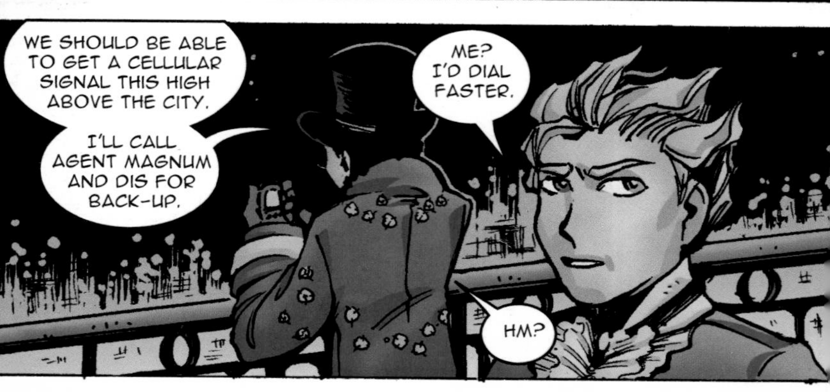
WE SHOULD BE ABLE TO GET A CELLULAR SIGNAL THIS HIGH ABOVE THE CITY.
I'LL CALL AGENT MAGNUM AND DIS FOR BACK-UP.
HM?
ME? I'D DIAL FASTER.

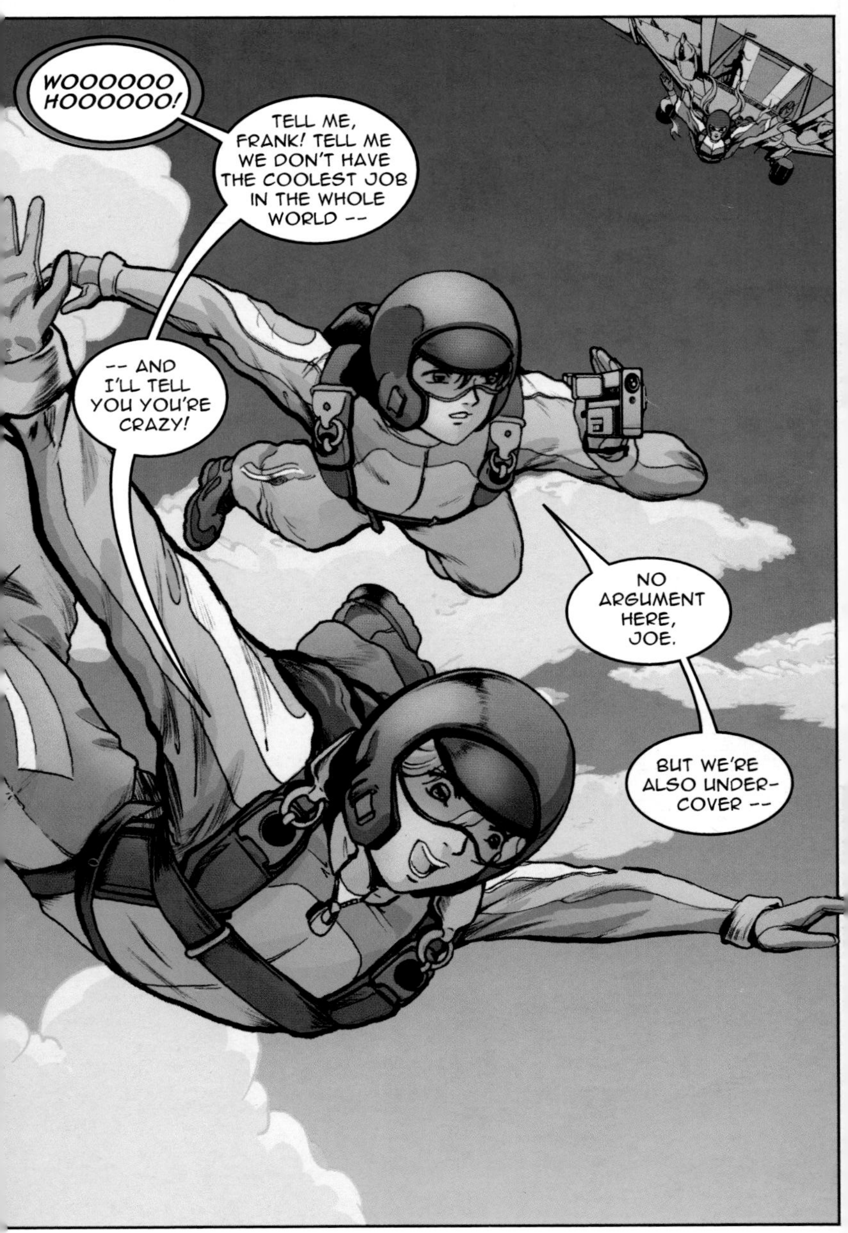
WOOOOOO HOOOOOO!
TELL ME, FRANK! TELL ME WE DON'T HAVE THE COOLEST JOB IN THE WHOLE WORLD --
-- AND I'LL TELL YOU YOU'RE CRAZY!
NO ARGUMENT HERE, JOE.
BUT WE'RE ALSO UNDER-COVER --

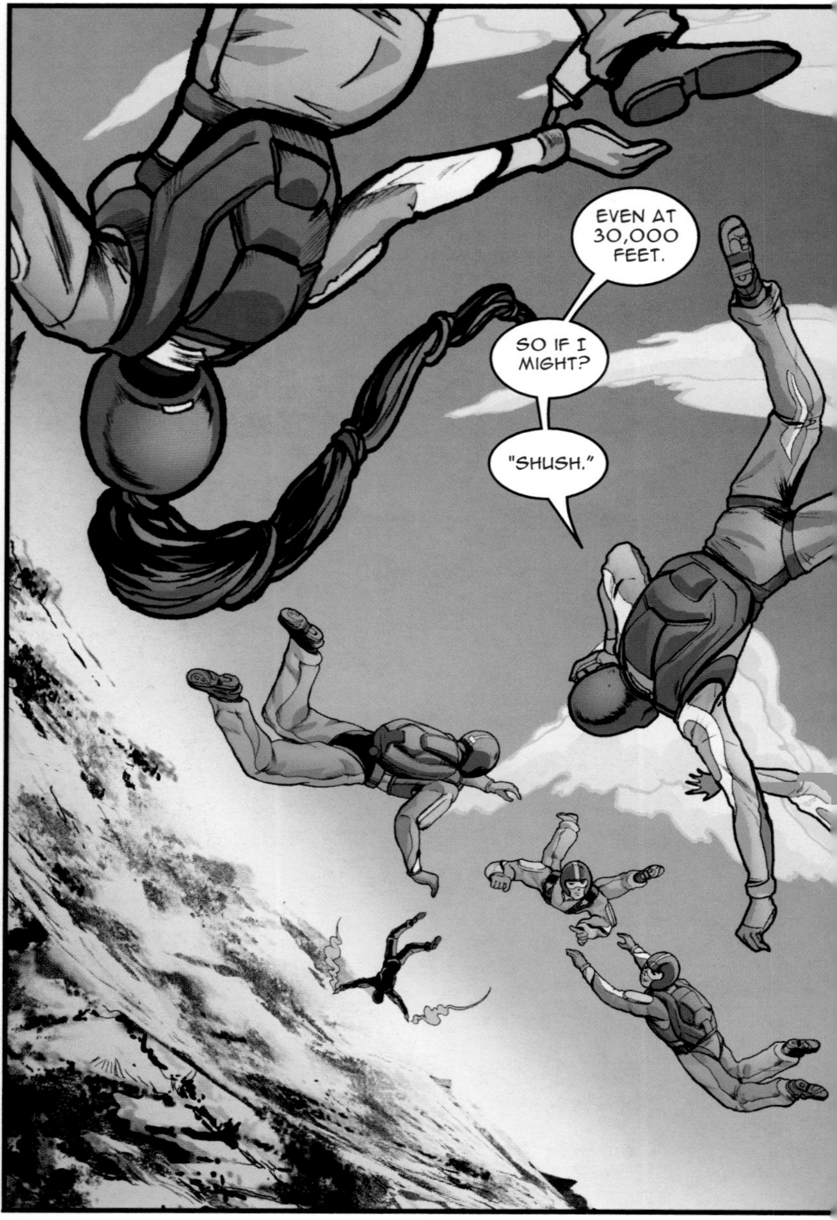
EVEN AT 30,000 FEET.
SO IF I MIGHT?
"SHUSH."

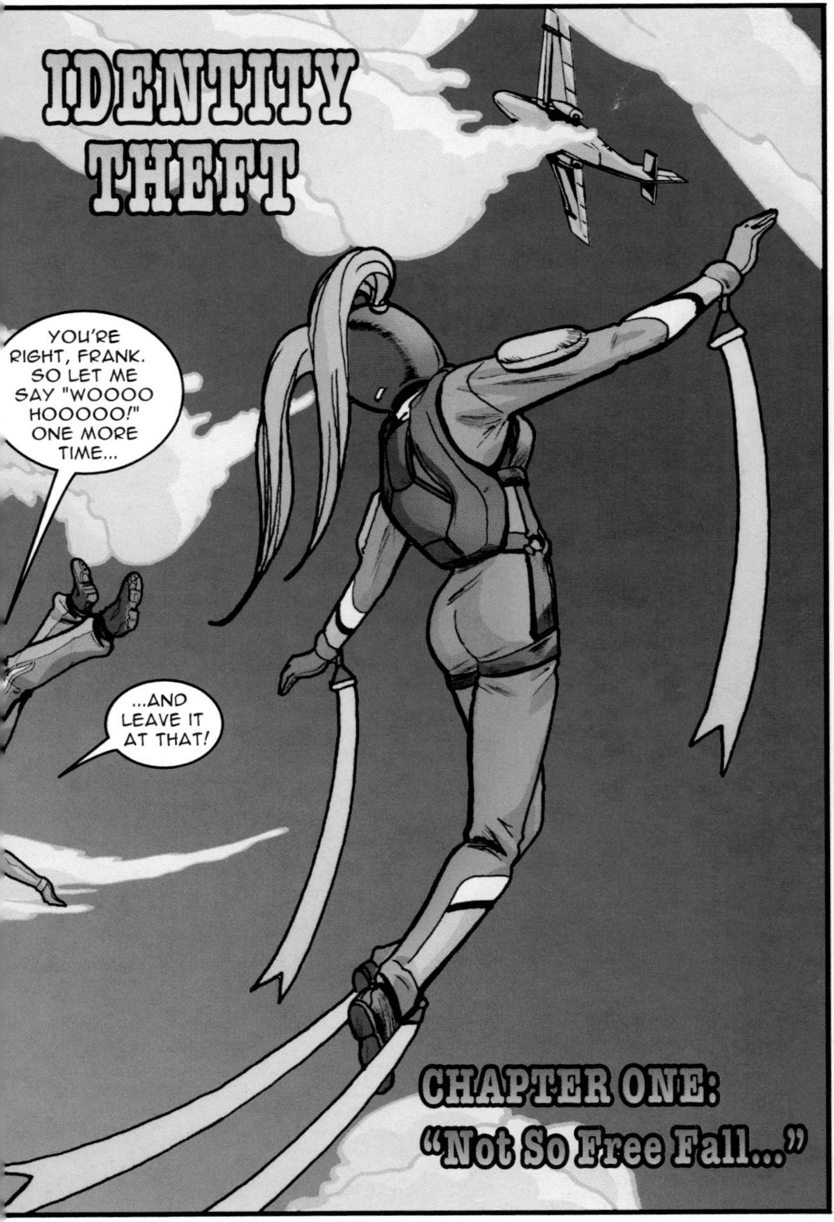
IDENTITY THEFT
YOU'RE RIGHT, FRANK. SO LET ME SAY "WOOOO HOOOOO!" ONE MORE TIME...
...AND LEAVE IT AT THAT!
CHAPTER ONE:
"Not So Free Fall..."

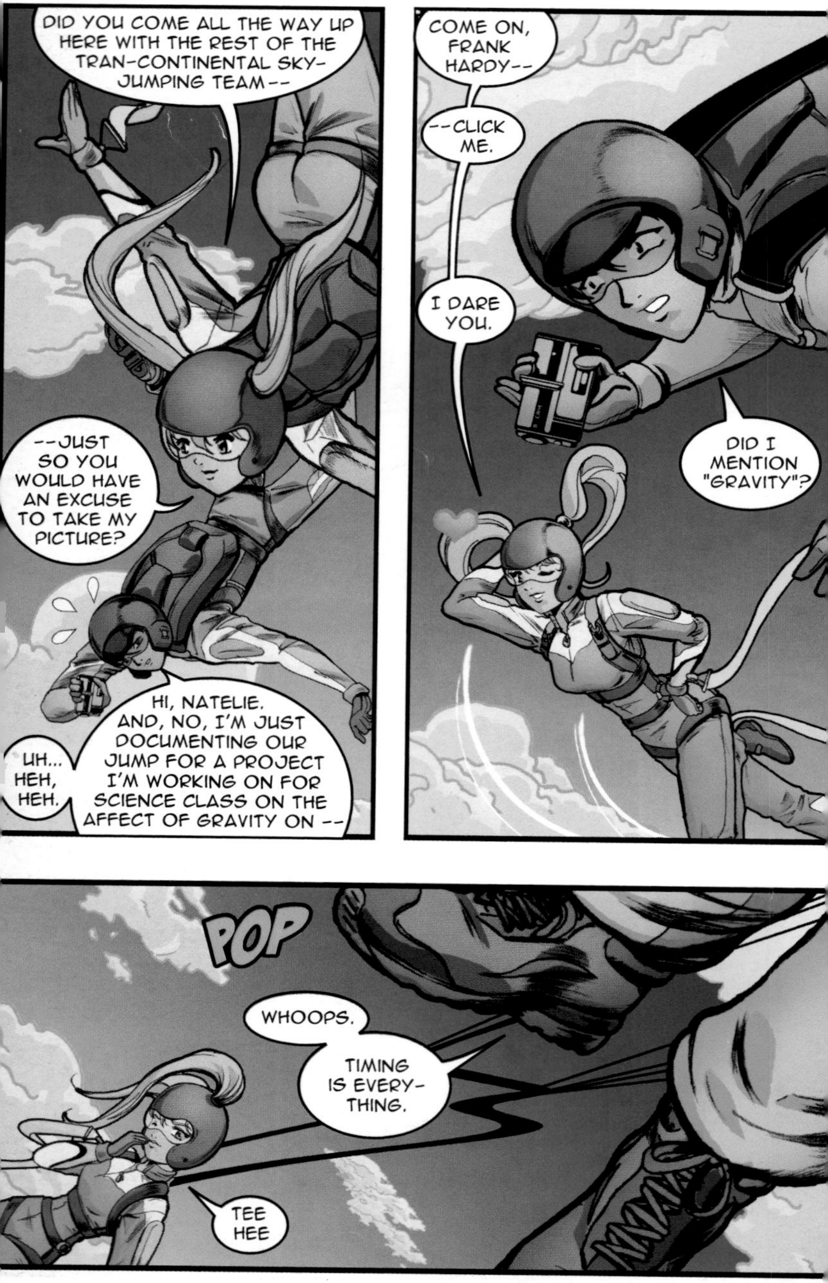
DID YOU COME ALL THE WAY UP HERE WITH THE REST OF THE TRAN-CONTINENTAL SKY-JUMPING TEAM --
--JUST SO YOU WOULD HAVE AN EXCUSE TO TAKE MY PICTURE?
UH... HEH, HEH.
HI, NATELIE. AND, NO, I'M JUST DOCUMENTING OUR JUMP FOR A PROJECT I'M WORKING ON FOR SCIENCE CLASS ON THE AFFECT OF GRAVITY ON --
COME ON, FRANK HARDY--
--CLICK ME.
I DARE YOU.
DID I MENTION "GRAVITY"?
POP
WHOOPS.
TIMING IS EVERY-THING.
TEE HEE

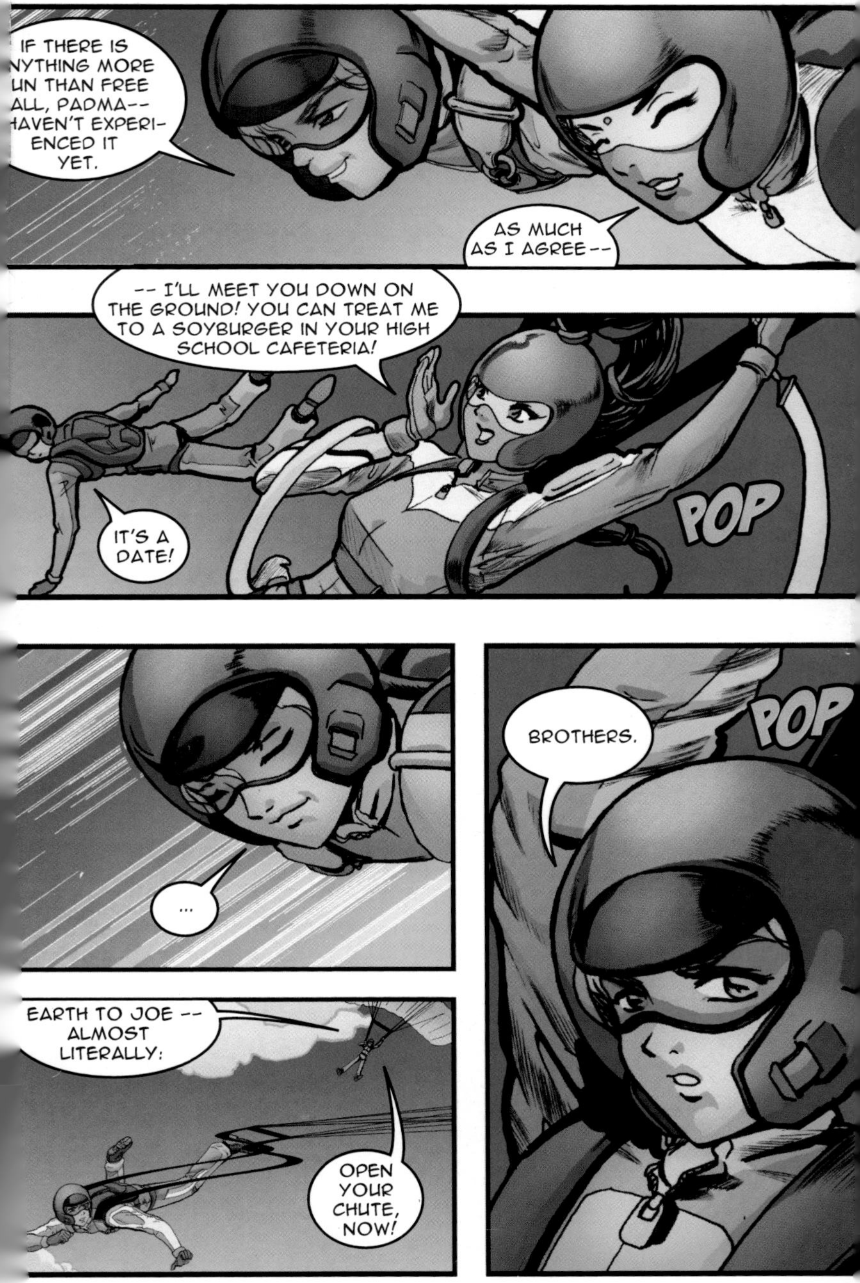
IF THERE IS
NYTHING MORE
UN THAN FREE
ALL, PADMA--
HAVEN'T EXPERI-
ENCED IT
YET.
AS MUCH
AS I AGREE--
-- I'LL MEET YOU DOWN ON
THE GROUND! YOU CAN TREAT ME
TO A SOYBURGER IN YOUR HIGH
SCHOOL CAFETERIA!
IT'S A
DATE!
POP
...
EARTH TO JOE --
ALMOST
LITERALLY:
OPEN
YOUR
CHUTE,
NOW!
BROTHERS.
POP

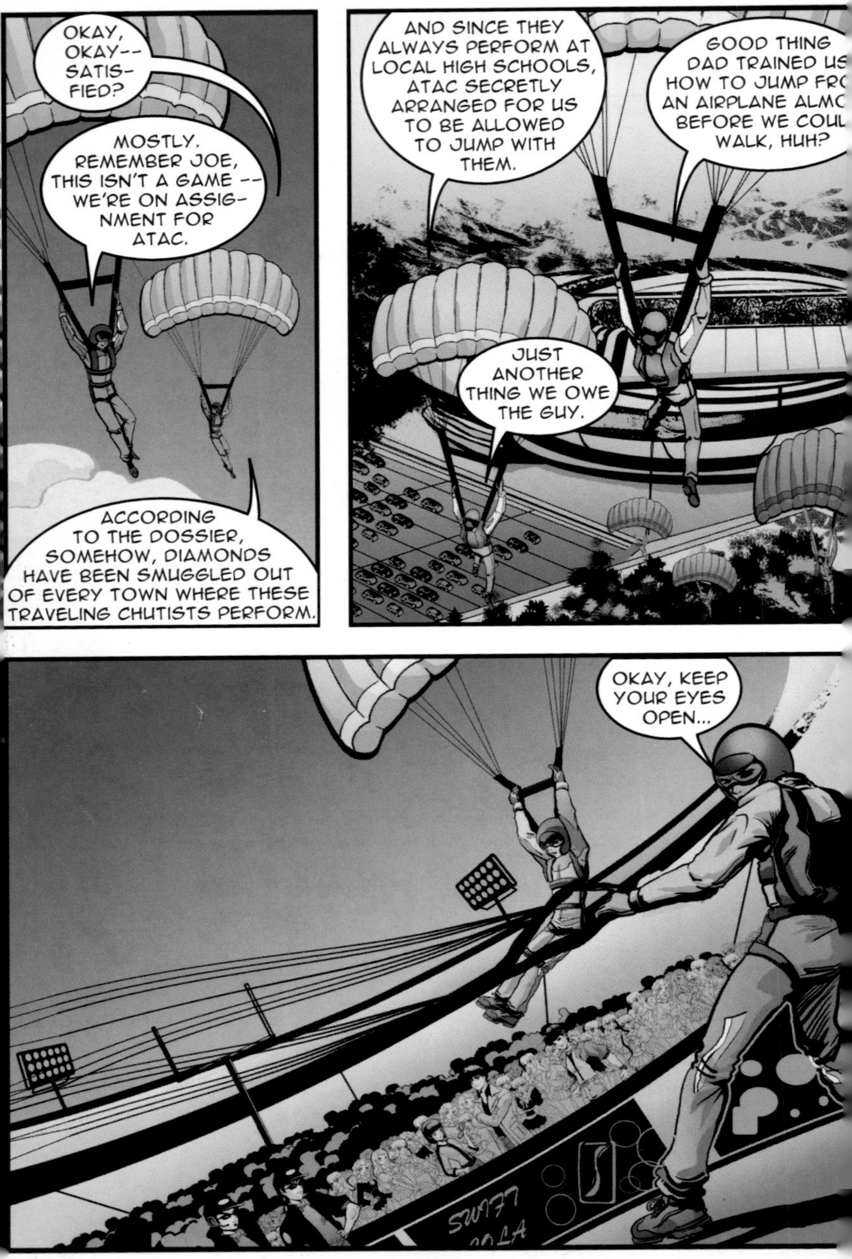
OKAY, OKAY-- SATIS- FIED?
MOSTLY. REMEMBER JOE, THIS ISN'T A GAME -- WE'RE ON ASSIG- NMENT FOR ATAC.
ACCORDING TO THE DOSSIER, SOMEHOW, DIAMONDS HAVE BEEN SMUGGLED OUT OF EVERY TOWN WHERE THESE TRAVELING CHUTISTS PERFORM.
AND SINCE THEY ALWAYS PERFORM AT LOCAL HIGH SCHOOLS, ATAC SECRETLY ARRANGED FOR US TO BE ALLOWED TO JUMP WITH THEM.
GOOD THING DAD TRAINED US HOW TO JUMP FRO AN AIRPLANE ALMO BEFORE WE COUL WALK, HUH?
JUST ANOTHER THING WE OWE THE GUY.
OKAY, KEEP YOUR EYES OPEN...

Don't miss THE HARDY BOYS Graphic Novel #2 – "Identity Theft"